MAGE'S STAFF

BOOK I: THRUST INTO BATTLE

DEZ ZURI

Maddeningly Erotic Books

Mage's Staff Book 1: Thrust into Battle
Copyright © 2026 Dez Zuri

All Rights Reserved

ISBN: 978-1-967517-14-5

Cover art:
Anxiety Driven Graphics

INTO THE FOLD

"THE HELL YOU do you mean we're stuck with him?"

It was a testament to his willpower that Guild official Geoffrey Dennen did not quake or tremble in the face of the furious, heavily armed and armored paladin in front of him. She was angry, but he was used to angry. He dealt with anger the way he dealt with everything: bureaucratic paperwork.

"You put in for a wizard," he said slowly and calmly, hoping his calm would ease the tension and she would follow suit.

"Witch or sorceress," she corrected.

"You put in for a caster," he returned, correcting her correction.

She leaned in close, her bright-green eyes darkening in rage. She was a hard woman, chiseled in the halls of her temple before being tempered in the heat of war. "A female caster," she growled.

"No, just a caster," he said softly, not breaking eye contact. She was formidable, but he was a Guild representative. Harming him would have dire consequences. He reached down and pulled out a yellowed envelope. "I have your request here if you would like to look over it."

She snatched it from his hand and snarled, baring her teeth at him. "I don't need to look over it. I know I explicitly explained that ours is an all-woman outfit."

"Yes, you did," the official conceded. "But we are aware of two other things, the first being that your last sorceress, chosen by you, broke contract and cost both you and the Guild dearly, meaning your judgment and rulings mean very little to the Guild. The second is, despite the lapse in judgment, there are very few troops with your track record for success—"

"That is due to our makeup. We do not suffer idiots or men," she said in a lowered tone, pacified by the admonishment from the official.

"And so we have seen fit to provide you with a phenomenal graduate of the Yolathian Academy. Top marks, best of his class," he finished.

"I don't accept him. Give me the second best, the third best, but give me a woman who will not disrupt—"

"The choice simply isn't yours to make, Captain Lakista. He is available now, and he has the skills necessary. As per Guild charter, all troops that see action against targets with magical capabilities must field at least one battle mage registered with the Academy. If you want to reject him, I will be forced to remove your active status."

"Or we simply don't take any jobs against foes with mages until we can get a sorceress," Lakista suggested.

"I see," the official said. He glanced around the small tent. The mage in question stood in silence. He didn't try to defend himself, and that was good. He doubted the young man could make things any better by butting in. Quiet and respectful—they trained them well in the Academy. "That could work. Of course, we would need to cancel your current deployment, as well as end your current contracted status with the Guild. Once we can find a suitable replacement, we would of course renegotiate the Defiant Host's contract."

"Renegotiate?" Lakista smirked. "I think that would go favorably for me, considering our track record."

"Yes, let's consider your track record. Remind me, who lost the battle of Fralt?"

The words were a whisper from Dennen, but Lakista reacted like he had struck her, reeling back. She had no answer for that. Fralt was the reason they were here; Fralt had been a crucible that had nearly broken the Defiant Host. Now, the Guild was holding that over her head, forcing her to take in this *boy*.

It wasn't a stalemate. He had won. And they both knew it. She had an indomitable willpower, but she would let nothing stand in the way of her company. Not even this.

She looked the mage over. He didn't look like he could handle a battle, but mages rarely did. His robes were a dark purple, a shimmering incandescence moving across them in the candlelight that lit the tent. Around his waist, he wore a thick chain as a belt, the chain lashed to an even thicker book—his spell book, she assumed. His hands were calloused and ink-stained, not as fine as some mages. His face, the only other part of the boy not covered by his voluminous robes, was graced with strong patrician features. At least he didn't look the part of a sickly plague victim like so many magic-users. She guessed he had grown up on a farm near a major city. Good. She had no use for those who were strangers to hard work. He didn't meet her eyes, keeping his head down, subdued. His hair— a muddy brown, she guessed, judging by his eyebrows—was shorn nearly to the scalp, standard practice of the Guild to ensure he would not bring lice to his new outfit.

For his part, he had traveled long hours over the road from Kandan, capital city of Estherfel, to join the company and was secretly relieved that he would not have to immediately head back on the road so soon.

"Fine," Lakista snarled, and marched back to her desk and put quill to paper, acknowledging the acceptance of the boy's contract. She looked over the contract one last time. It was a surrender of sorts, a defeat. It made her furious. "But only until such a time as we can have a suitable replacement sent. You understand?"

"Perfectly, Captain," the official said as he took the signed contract from her. "We will keep our eyes open for a suitable replacement, one who meets . . . both of our requirements." He started to leave and then paused. "Of course, should young master Dhalius meet some unfortunate accident or perfectly preventable mishap on the battlefield, we would have to consider that when it came time to renew your contracts. I am sure you also understand perfectly." He continued on his way, nodding his head to the mage as he left him in the woman's care.

"Mage," Captain Lakista finally said, as though the word was something disgusting she had taken a bite of that needed to be spit out.

"Yes, ma'am."

"You mean 'yes, Captain.'" Lakista corrected.

"Yes, Captain," Dhali agreed. This was not looking great for him. He had assumed he would be placed with his sisters' company. He had traveled with them before, had requested them, and knew they had put in a request for a mage at the same time. But just like Captain Lakista, his preferences meant little to the Guild.

She stared at him for a few more minutes. "It pains me to say this, mage, but as much as I don't want you here, we do need a caster. So instead of sitting you somewhere out of sight where you can languish and do chores in exchange for food and water, I'm going to include you in our actions. It will give you an opportunity to prove yourself."

"Thank you, Captain," Dhali responded dutifully.

"Don't thank me. You'll prove yourself worthwhile or die in battle and I can request another caster." She held his gaze for another moment, her eyes offering no mercy or solace. Finally, she looked away, moving back to her desk. "Neela!" she barked.

A second later, a woman entered the tent. She was a stark contrast to the captain. Where the captain was an intimidating warrior cut from marble who nearly towered above Dhali in her armor, this new woman was slender and smaller than Dhali. She wore a thin white slip of silk that seemed to be nearly translucent, revealing her earthen-brown skin beneath when light from a candle caught it from behind. Her features were fine to the point of delicacy beneath the thick green curls that made up her hair.

Lakista glanced up and nodded towards Dhali. "Take him to a tent, get him set up."

"Tori?" Neela asked.

Lakista's head snapped up, her eyes narrowing in warning. "The Guild has spoken and promised to remedy the situation as quickly as possible. Now take him to a tent."

Neela nodded and pushed through the tent opening into the warm night, gliding along the ground as graceful as any courtroom dancer. Dhali bowed to Lakista and then hurried to follow Neela. She was waiting for him just outside the tent.

"These are yours, I assume?" She gestured to the pack and large trunk that the Guild had offloaded.

"Ah yes. Those are my belongings." He hurried to pull the pack on and grab the handle of the trunk. It had been a gift from his mother when he left for the Academy, a rolling trunk capable of carrying his meager wardrobe and, more importantly, the tools of his chosen profession. "Okay, lead the—" he started, but she was already walking away. He took a moment to admire the shape of her as the moonlight shone through her slip, revealing the gentle curves of her body as she moved, then hurried after.

She silently led him through the camp. He didn't mind the silence as he took in his new "home." The camp was a temporary one. His understanding was that the Defiant Host was a nomadic troop, carrying their homes with them from battlefield to battlefield. He caught glimpses of mercenaries and soldiers moving through the camp, women going about their business, preparing for war. He had heard of the Defiant Host; it was one of the companies his sisters had spoken of joining before they had been assigned. The fact that he was now stationed with the Host instead of his sisters was odd—seeing as they had requested the Host and he had requested their company—but he was determined to prove his worth to his new troop.

Dhali nearly ran into Neela, so distracted by taking in the camp that he hadn't noticed she'd stopped in front of a small tent. She stared at him, seemingly bored, before she pulled open the tent flap and ushered him in. He followed her into the tent, dragging his trunk. Inside, it was nearly pitch black. Dhali carefully set his belongings down, opening his eyes wide in an effort to make out the interior.

Suddenly, a soft blue light blinded Dhali, and he let out a surprised yelp right before he realized Neela had summoned a floating glowing orb that hovered just above her lifted hand. She raised an eyebrow at him in obvious judgment.

"Sorry," he mumbled, embarrassed, "I wasn't expecting—" He paused, realizing. "Magic. You're a caster. So why—"

"Are you here?" she finished for him. "I'm not a battle mage; I am an Alarune and one of the company's healers. My magic can only soothe and heal; we need someone who can kill. You can kill, can't you?"

Dhali opened his mouth and then closed it again. He was trained to kill with magic, and he had learned to use both a mace and a dagger in close combat. But he had never taken a life. He would need to, he had to, if he couldn't, then it would be his life that was ended. Slowly, he nodded.

"Good, go ahead and disrobe," Neela commanded.

"What?"

"Take. Off. Your. Clothes," she clarified slowly, as though he were slow.

"No, I—I heard you. Why?" he asked.

"Because it is my job to carry out your physical inspection, to ensure you are not bringing disease or illness into our camp, to ensure you are actually in fighting shape," she explained, the bored expression not leaving her face.

Dhali swallowed. She had perfectly valid reasons and a reasonable explanation, but still, getting undressed in front of a stranger—especially a beautiful stranger who was wearing only a thin translucent gown—was intimidating. But he was determined to show that he wouldn't prove the captain right and make his sex a liability to the company. He reached down and unclasped the heavy chains that kept his book attached to his body and carefully set the book and its chain on top of the trunk. He gave her one last look to make sure she wasn't making him a fool before reaching down and then pulling his robes over his head, leaving himself nude in front of her.

Neela trailed her eyes over his body, the same bored expression on her face, although he could have sworn he saw the smallest smile flit across her mouth. She stepped forward, the glowing orb staying put. Dhali almost stepped back but thought better of it. Her hands, soft and gentle, touched his chest, trailing over the definition of his pecs and running over his shoulders.

"You know work. You aren't just a scholar," she said.

"I trained for war . . . and worked the fields near the university," he said, keeping his eyes up and to the left, willing his body to not react to her presence. His will was faltering, and he could feel his erection rising as her hands explored him.

"Good," she remarked, close enough that he could feel her breath on his neck as her hands dipped, running over his ribs and across his stomach.

Dhali held his breath, biting his tongue and wishing fervently that his raging hard-on would magically calm down.

"Turn," she ordered.

Dhali didn't hesitate, glad for the excuse to aim his throbbing member away from her. He sighed in relief as he felt her hands on his back.

"I have to admit," she said almost conversationally, "I was not expecting you to have any meat on your bones. I was expecting you to be a sickly waif of a man."

"Oh," Dhali said, unsure how to respond. He knew why she had expected that; most of his colleagues had been just so. "I try to remain healthy. I believe a healthy body aids in a strong mi—" He choked off as he felt her reach around and grip his engorged cock.

He sucked in a breath, trying to ignore the coolness of her hands against the heat of his body and the way her small, firm breasts were now pressed into his back. Slowly, she starting stroking his cock with firm, smooth motions. He swallowed and looked down. The low light from the glowing globe behind him barely illuminated her actions, but he could just see the shape of her lithe hand moving up and down his shaft.

"What are you doing?" he hissed through his teeth, afraid of shouting.

"Mmmh," she breathed in his ear, her other hand moving around his hip and cupping his balls. Slowly, she gently kneaded his testes, making him shudder. "Testing your stamina. Do you want me to stop?" Her voice was husky, hints of teasing hidden in her whisper.

He bit his lip to keep from moaning. He couldn't answer as she continued her gentle massage of his shaft. Her hands moved almost expertly, gliding across his skin to slide over the tip of his cock and back down. He felt her teeth graze his neck. He stared down, watching her deft movements as her hands became wet, lubricated with precum.

"Neela . . ." he whispered. "Neela, if you keep going . . ."

"I can feel it," she whispered back. "I can feel the tightness, the heat. Go on. Do it," she ordered, increasing the pressure and speed.

Dhali gritted his teeth. He wanted to hold on, but it was too much. The vision of her hands stroking him, her body against his back, her breath in his ear . . . He came hard, riding the orgasm as it rushed through his body. His knees nearly gave out, and he leaned back against Neela to keep from falling over. For her part, she didn't slow down, continuing to slide her hand up and down his shaft as he ejaculated across the floor of his tent.

Finally, Neela released him and stepped away.

Dhali staggered and leaned against his trunk, panting softly. He looked up at the healer. She was looking down at her hand. She glanced at him, and, maintaining eye contact, brought her hand up and ran her tongue over her fingers, lapping up his cum. She swallowed without looking away and then nodded, more to herself than anything. Then the bored expression she had worn throughout the walk here returned, and she stepped past him.

"Clean up the mess and get some rest, mage. Tomorrow, you join the company formally." And with that, she left, plunging the tent back into darkness and leaving Dhali panting and at a loss.

PENNED IN BLOOD

THE BLARING SOUND of a trumpet yanked Dhali roughly from his fitful rest. After Neela had left his tent, he had done his best to kick dirt from the floor of the tent over the mess he had made, then wrapped himself in his robes and collapsed into the small cot that had been provided. It wasn't comfortable, and without unpacking his belongings, he couldn't make it more so, but its simple metal frame kept it off the ground, and he was so exhausted from his travel and encounter that he decided to simply try to sleep.

He rolled off the cot and slowly pulled himself up, too used to the beds and slow mornings of Academy now—he regretted not putting in for a cushy city job. Dhali moved to his trunk as the trumpet continued its clarion call across the camp, and pushed it open. Inside was the sum of his belongings now. He pulled out a fresh robe and pulled it over his head, then fastened the chain with his spell book around his waist. He realized belatedly that in the rush of last night's . . . encounters, he had forgotten to ask anything about routine. What time was mess? Was there a stream where he could get clean? What chores would be assigned to him? He grimaced, certain this would bite him in the ass.

Stepping out of his small tent, Dhali was greeted by the sight of the camp coming to life. Women were emerging from their own tents in droves, pulling on armor, fastening weapons and gear as they moved. He stood at the mouth of his own pitiful lodgings for a moment, taking in the sight of the sun rising over the camp.

"You are the new mage?" a strangely ethereal voice asked to his right.

"Ah, yes," he answered, turning to face the speaker, a blond Elvish woman who only came up to his chest. Despite her short stature, the Elf looked like she could, and would, easily kill Dhali if she decided she didn't care for him. She wore a leather corset and skirt over leggings and carried a fine Elvish bow over her shoulder. He knew of the Elvish rangers but had never seen one in person. "I am Dhalius, it's nice to—"

"You sound like a human. And a man," she interrupted.

"Well, yes, I am."

"Gross," she said, wrinkling her nose in disgust. She began walking away, in the same direction Dhali noticed all the other women walking. She paused and glanced over her shoulder at him, still looking annoyed. "Man or not, if you are joining the company in battle, you ought to make haste. Captain Lakista will be issuing orders." With that, she continued on her way.

Dhali's stomach growled. He was hungry as sin, but considering the piss-poor impression he had managed to make so far—on everyone other than Neela at least—he decided not to inquire about breakfast and hastened to follow the ranger towards the center of camp.

Captain Lakista was already speaking to the rapidly assembled company of mercenaries when Dhali caught up to the group. He glanced around quickly and saw there were plenty of others still joining the gathering in the space. All around him were women armed and armored for war, but there was no unified armor for those gathered. He saw leather armor as well as chainmail and platemail. Weapons that met every possible description. It seemed that if it had been designed to kill or protect from being killed, the women of the Defiant Host wielded and wore it. It was also the greatest gathering of diverse races he had seen in one place before. Elves, humans, and Dwarves he expected. But he spotted Goblins, scaled humanoids with reptilian features, vegetation-covered Dryads, and many more he couldn't easily identify.

"The enemy is the House of Rotting Eaves. A necromantic cult that is trying to wrest power from the good peoples of Zachman's Crossing," Lakista was saying—Zachman's Crossing was a larger settlement, teetering between being a town and a city, full of a few hundred families; their loss would be a terrible tragedy and would swell an undead army's size at the same time. "While this may seem like a skirmish, and a minor one at that, we will be dealing with two factors that make this more dangerous. First is that our enemy has been raising the dead of the slain to join their ranks, so we will be outnumbered."

"Not outclassed!" a Dwarf shouted from the crowd; she wore thick plates of interlocking shimmering armor. A small cheer rose from around her, and Captain Lakista smiled and nodded—it was the first time Dhalius had seen her express anything other than irritation.

"No, not outclassed. Never outclassed. That does bring us to the second part. We have to assume they have at least one if not several necromancers in their midst, mages who will bend their spells and skills at killing and raising us to fight for them."

There was a general murmur of anger at her words.

"Fucking mages," Dhalius heard someone curse from behind him, but he didn't want to turn to see who it was, especially after he heard the grunted assent at the words from others. Lakista held up a hand to silence the talking.

"Our healers and clerics will be at the forefront. Prepare your protective spells; prepare to sever the connection between the walking corpses and the magic that keeps them up. And on that note, I am sure many of you are already aware that we have a stranger in our midst."

Dhalius swallowed, lowering his head, wishing he had pulled the hood up so no one could see how brightly he blushed at being called out.

"The Guild has seen fit to fulfill our request for a new caster. They have sent a . . . man," Lakista finished.

A silence fell over the assembled company. And then, just as suddenly, an outcry. Protests, questions, shouts, and chaos. Several women turned to stare at him. He imagined they were glowering, but he kept his eyes down, wishing he could shrink into his robes and disappear.

"Enough! I'm no happier than you, but without a mage, we lose our charter. So we make do. Understood?" She paused and glared over the assembled women. Her eyes fell on Dhali. "Mage, now is your chance to prove to all of us that you're worth more than the weight of your skin. Your magic against theirs. You'll be on the front lines." She waited to see if Dhali would dare object to the assignment. When he remained silent, she continued. "Korska! You and yours will guard the casters; make sure no one gets close enough to bruise them." From across the field, Dhali heard the gruff shout of affirmation. Satisfied, Lakista finished. "Everyone else, we'll be following the Dorsen deployment. If you have questions, or concerns, or if you have not yet fought the undead, come see myself or Neela as we march. Dismissed."

Dhali was relieved there was indeed a morning mess served. He took his food and returned to his tent to eat, painfully aware of the eyes on him as he moved through the camp. He hoped he could run into Neela—after last night, surely, she was at least more ambivalent than the others? But she was nowhere to be seen, and he had to assume she was with Captain Lakista, a presence he would like to avoid if at all possible. He also wanted to meet

Korska and her unit—if they were going to defend him, he should get to know them—but Dhali had no way of knowing who the woman was. So he just hurried back to enjoy his rations.

He was mid-meal when the sound of the trumpet erupted outside. Dhali ducked his head out of the tent and saw the entire camp was once again assembling, this time to march.

He sighed and hurried to join the throng of women, many of whom were trying to eat their own breakfasts as they moved. He fell into step beside them, trying to stay out of the way. Dhalius wasn't sure where he was expected to be, but if he was to fight on the front lines, he should try to get to the front of the formation.

Moving through the crowd was a challenge in and of itself. The women had not grown kinder or more tolerant of his presence since the early morning briefing. But he managed to get to the front of the formation and saw Neela and Lakista leading the column of warriors. From the robes and staffs he was seeing around him, he imagined many of these women were clerics and healers. He settled into a steady pace, keeping abreast with the healers as the Defiant Host marched to war.

They arrived on the battlefield, just south of the town of Zachman's Crossing, with mere minutes to spare. Dhali did his best to stay out of the way as the women moved into position, forming a line of defense between the oncoming undead horde and the town. A cadre of gargantuan women in heavy plate armor, wielding massive swords and axes, moved into position around the casters. Dhali saw one woman barking orders for them. Easily over two meters in height, the woman sported a short black mohawk, olive green skin, and small tusks that jutted from beneath her bottom lip. An Orc! Korska was an Orc!

Dhali stared for a moment, having never seen an Orc

so close before, and never a female Orc in person at all. But before he could really process the sight, a horrendous screech split the air, tearing his attention away from the formidable woman to focus on the enemy. The undead horde was advancing. Dhali had heard of them, of zombies, of course—he had studied the history of necromancy at the Academy—but the reality was so much more horrifying. The rotting faces showed no signs of the hunger or feral rage he had expected. They were dull and lifeless, pocked with maggot-filled rotting wounds. A putrid tide of reaching claws and rusted weapons, behind which Dhali could sense the presence of foul magic that made bile rise in his throat.

He had no more time to gawk and study the enemy as, with a shout, the Defiant Host surged forward, blade meeting claw in a chaos Dhali had only understood on an intellectual level before. As with the undead, the reality was far more overwhelming. Everywhere he looked, violence was taking place. The women around him were unfazed, grim scowls meeting the unfeeling dead as they parried and delivered brutal ripostes to their foes.

"Oi!"

Dhalius felt a tug on his robes. Looking down, he was surprised to see a small Goblin woman in a brown robe, with massive pointed ears festooned with dangling rings and chains. She was moss green with strange yellow stripes across the skin he could see, had oversized gold-yellow eyes, and a mouth that seemed too large for her face filled with large, sharp teeth.

"If you gonna prove yourself, stop gawkin' and start slingin' spells!" she shouted over the cacophony of battle.

"Shit!" Dhali spat, realizing he had been so taken by the sight of the Defiant Host battling the undead that he had forgotten that he was no spectator. "Thank you!" he whispered to the small woman and lifted his book up into his hands. He was already intoning the words of his spells as the book fell open in his palm, revealing pages that were soaked in ink. Solid blacks, purples, and reds, with no words writ on any of the pages. Arcane power filled him as he gathered his will. Purple light spilling from his eyes, he shouted the final word of his binding spell and lifted his free hand above his head.

The ink of his book pulled itself from the pages, flowing up in a multihued stream, then began to take the shape of a large wolf. The ink-wolf leapt from its perch into the air and landed among the dead, tearing them apart with jaws that possessed the crushing power of a steel trap. Rotting bones cracked and maggots spilled to the ground as the dye-constructed beast ripped apart the enemy, trailing gangrenous intestines and papery flesh in its wake.

"Oh hell!" Dhali heard the Goblin whisper at his waist, but he couldn't pull his attention away from his creation.

The undead attacked it with blades, but the ink simply parted like water and reformed after the attack. Dhali pushed the ink-wolf deep behind enemy lines and spread his arms apart. The ink-wolf exploded out, flinging the dead across the battlefield in broken heaps.

An undead figure, easily three meters tall, broke through the line of warriors and charged towards the casters, swinging a massive mace. Dhali began trying to reweave the ink into some form he could control, but the monstrosity was already amongst them. Korska stepped forward, using her axe to deflect the blow. The two titans battled it out as Dhali tried to gain control of his spell. The axe and maul met between the combatants, but with each strike, Korska showed more signs of fatigue, whereas the zombie had no such limits.

With another blow, the giant knocked Korska's axe aside and lifted his maul above his head to crush the Orc. Dhali shouted and swung his fist around, directing the unformed ink back from the battlefield. The dark glimmering liquid flowed through the air and slammed into the monstrosity, wrapping around it like a cloak. Dhali gestured, pulling the giant off the ground and suspending him above the battlefield. Sweat pouring from his brow, Dhali pulled the ink tight around the creature and began ripping him apart, the ink grabbing and yanking at rotting flesh, tearing the skin and muscle apart and flinging the now inanimate parts back into the field of battle.

"Keep pushing!"

He heard Lakista's voice over the din. Panting, he turned his eyes back towards the battle. Where would he be most useful? There! He saw one of the necromancers, an ugly and unkempt man with a straggly beard and wild eyes. His hands waved above his head, directing foul green energy around the battle, raising his minions and shooting darts of foul necrotic energy towards the Host.

Dhali stepped towards the vile caster and pushed his hand forward as if throwing a ball as hard as he could. The ink, noticeably smaller now than at the beginning of the battle, launched through the horde of undead, bowling them over or punching through their rotten torsos. As it reached the necromancer, the ink took the shape of a man, albeit a man formed of ever shifting fluid.

Dhali leapt forward, the ink mimicking his movements and grappling the man's hands down to his side. Dhali could only barely see the man through the throng of the battle, but he needed to stop him from casting. Dhali leaned back and brought his head forward, slamming his simulacrum's forehead into the necromancer's face. He could feel the impact through his spell; his head split open where the necromancer's teeth cut into his skin. But the evil mage fell. Dhalius stumbled, stars swimming in his vision, but he maintained his feet, wrapping his spell around the fallen man and dragging him, wrapped in ink, through the chaotic battle, back behind the Defiant Host's line.

REFRESHED

"**B**EST THING ABOUT the undead?" Korska was saying as the casters were trying to regain their footing after the battle. "They don't give up, they don't retreat, so you can exterminate them all."

"They did retreat," one of the armored women retorted.

"That's the necromancers. The cult retreated; their fodder, not so much." Korska snorted, she was about to go on when Lakista's voice rang out over the field.

"Korska, Vamithin, gather our wounded and fallen, burn the rest. The rest of you, head back to camp!"

The Host let out a shout of confirmation and began to once again move.

Dhalius was sweaty and exhausted. He couldn't fathom the march back to camp, but there were precious few other options. He pulled himself up from where he had collapsed after the battle and started the long trek back. As he walked, he opened the book that hung from his waist and scowled at the number of now blank white pages. He had expended too much ink during the battle. He would need to carefully reconstruct his book before he was deployed again.

"Not bad for a first battle!" a voice said from about waist high.

Dhali glanced over and saw the Goblin walking next to him—her short legs had to be working twice as hard under her robes to keep up. Now that there wasn't a battle going on, he took the time to look her over. She was an attractive woman, though her eyes and mouth were much larger than they would be on a human her size. Beyond all the jewelry attached to her ears, he now saw there were just as many chains and straps across her robes, each littered with bottles, vials, and pouches.

"You're an alchemist?" Dhalius asked, suddenly excited.

"If you want to call it that. It isn't what I call it, but I understand how things come together and what happens then," she retorted, stretching and rubbing her shoulder as they walked. "Why?"

"Can you make inks and paints?"

"Ah," she said, peering up at him and his book. "For your magic?"

He nodded.

"Prolly! I'm Ten-Tulips, by the way."

"Oh, Dhal—"

"Dhalius, I know. Was there for the announcement, and word travels fast. Welcome to the Host," Ten said with a smile that looked positively predatory.

"Thank you."

"How you like it so far?" she asked.

Dhali was taken aback by the exuberance of the Goblin, but it was a far cry better than the cold shoulder or outright malice the others had shown him so far. He decided he would rather have an overly noisy friend than a silent walk by himself.

"It's strange, not what I expected when I joined the Guild," he admitted. "But, impressive. It's more ordered than other mercenary outfits I've traveled with, more diverse by a long shot."

"Never met a Gob' before?" Ten asked.

"Uh, no, actually. I've seen Goblins before, in the city, but never had a conversation or fought next to one," he admitted. "Or Orcs, for that matter. Or any number of the soldiers I saw at the assembly."

"Eh, a lot of merc outfits want to specialize. They say, oh this outfit for *humans* or *we only take Elven rangers*, or usually just *no green skins!*" She paused to pull a canteen out of her robe and took a mighty gulp.

"The Defiant Host isn't entirely different. It specializes by only accepting women, right?" Dhalius asked.

"Eh. 'pearantly not," she said, grinning and reaching up to poke him in the side. "But you're right; but we don't discriminate on other things. So long as you can follow orders and pull your weight in and out of a fight, the Lakistas will accept you." She grinned again, shooting him a sideways look. "Pretty exciting for you, though, eh?"

"How do you mean?" he asked, unsure if she was suggesting something lewd.

"Defiant Host is best mercenary outfit, dozens of different cultures and tactics. No better place to be and learn. Most humans never get this opportunity, and no men. You lucked out." She looked up at him as though that should be obvious.

"I suppose so." It was a different way of looking at it; sure, this post might be temporary, but it was a fantastic opportunity. "Thank you, Ten-Tulips."

The two of them chatted as they walked, helping ease the hardship of the march. As they came upon the camp, Dhalius sighed.

"You said there was a river nearby? Somewhere I could get clean?"

"Yes, yes, most the Host will go northeast to the river and falls; is good location," Ten responded.

"Okay, if I just go east, though, I'll get to the river?" he asked. "And maybe avoid the others?"

She looked at him oddly, as if confused as to why he would possibly pass on the communal bath, but nodded.

"Great, thank you, Ten. I'll meet up with you later." And without waiting for her reply, he peeled from the main column and headed east.

He had only been walking for a few minutes when he heard the sound of the bubbling river. He hoped he was far enough south to avoid the soldiers of the Host—and far enough north to avoid any residents of Zachman's Crossing. When he reached the edge of the river, Dhali looked around. He couldn't see or hear anyone else. He could just spot smoke rising from the direction of the battlefield, where the bodies of the undead were being burned, but otherwise, he was surrounded only by the woods and the flowing water.

Dhalius sighed and pulled his robes off over his head. The sweat from the march and the incredible strain of magic caused the dirt and grime of the road to cling to him. He folded his clothes, setting them on one of the nearby stones, and slowly stepped into the water, wincing at the sudden coolness of it. He took a few minutes to get used to the temperature before wading out further and diving under, letting the water wash over him and through his hair. It was bracing and refreshing.

Dhali swam, stretching his arms and legs, letting the weightlessness of the water soothe his muscles while he considered Ten's words. Considering this deployment as an opportunity to learn from other cultures and learn what made the Host so successful would help him get the most out of his time here . . . until Lakista got her way and he was sent somewhere else. He surfaced and leaned his back against a large rock near the bank of the river, lifting his hands from the water to look at his fingers. The ink wasn't coming off. It always took days to fully wash away, leaving his fingers and knuckles stained a multicolored hue until then.

"Clean yet?"

The sudden gruff question nearly made Dhali jump out

of his skin. Turning, he saw the massive armored frame of Korska standing just a few feet from him on the bank. He swiftly ducked to his shoulders in the water.

"I . . . I thought you all went further north," he stammered.

"Usually. But Ten said you came here. So I came here," she responded. Her voice wasn't anything like he would have imagined an Orcish voice to be. It was feminine despite having a harsh steely quality.

Dhali didn't know how to respond that, a bit nervous that the Orcish warrior had specifically been looking for him.

Korska moved, pulling her axe from its sheath and setting it against a nearby tree, then bent down at the waist to begin untying her boots.

Dhalius watched her, unsure if he should get dressed and go or stay put.

"Help me out of this armor," Korska said, suddenly straightening back up and kicking off one boot and then the other.

"Help you out of your armor?" Dhalius asked.

"Did I stumble over my words, mage? I'm not going to get in the water with it on." She gave him a sardonic smile made lopsided by her tusks. He was surprised by how attractive the expression looked on her face. He was especially startled by how breathtaking her eyes were, a strange mix of ochre yellows and deep browns, giving her eyes an almost golden hue.

"Well I'm not—I'm not dressed," he protested.

"I would think it odd if you were," she responded.

Dhali decided that maybe modesty was alien to the Orcs. Swallowing his nerves, he rose from his crouching spot and approached the larger woman.

"Ah, see, no need to be shy." She chuckled, eying him as he rose. "No, you have no reason to be shy at all, do you?"

Dhalius didn't answer, feeling the blush burning hot

across his shoulders and down his chest. He looked over Korska's armor for the latches and ties that were keeping it on and worked quickly to undo those he found. When he was finished, he stepped back and moved to grab his robes.

"Hold on," Korska commanded. "I'm not done with your help."

Dhali nodded and glanced over his shoulder at the Orc. She was pulling off the armor plate, leaving her in only a cloth chest wrap and a leather skirt. She was an intimidating figure even out of her armor, her muscled frame seemingly cut from jade. Every muscle on the woman was toned and defined, putting any human male he had ever encountered to shame. Her cut form certainly made him feel small and weak standing near her. At the same time, he was surprised at how attractive the muscular build was on the woman. He had never thought about muscular women being sexy before, but here and now, he couldn't deny the appeal. He bit his tongue, realizing that in his current state of undress, arousal would be a very evident state.

She pulled the leather skirt off, revealing cloth underwear. She closed her eyes and sighed in relief as the final bit of armor fell to the ground. Then she started pulling on her chest wrap. Dhali looked away, feeling awkward, but looked back as she let out another sigh, and nearly gasped. Without her chest wrap on, her heavy breasts were free, and they were each easily the size of Dhali's head. Each orb was tipped with a pale-green nipple sporting an ivory ring that caused it to stand at attention.

"Yes?" Korska asked, a sly grin on her face as she turned to face him.

How could someone with such a hard body sport such soft and inviting breasts? Dhali burned red as he hurried back to the water and dove in, praying the cold water would arrest his growing hard-on, or at least hide it from Korska's eyes. It did nothing to blunt his aching erection. Especially as she followed him in.

Her mohawk lost its form, falling to the left, draping across her eye as she rose back out of the water and began cleaning her skin. "The rinse after battle is always the best, isn't it?" she asked, doing nothing to hide her body.

Dhali stayed huddled in the water, unsure what his part in all of this was.

"It is, yes," he finally said, getting his voice under control. If she was going to act as if this were nothing strange or untoward, then by the gods, so would he. So long as he stayed with his waist under the water and his throbbing cock out of sight, there would be nothing out of the ordinary.

"Come, wash my back." She turned away from him, giving him a perfect view of her round, pert ass, muscular back, and myriad scars.

Dhali nodded and waded forward. He could do this. He reached out and rubbed his hand across her back, silently marveling at the warm, smooth hardness of her muscles. "You look so different than the Orcs I've seen in texts," he said, trying to sound casual, conversational.

"Let me guess." She glanced over her shoulder down at him. "You were expecting a big belly and pig features."

"Well . . . " Dhali realized he had probably offended the giant woman and she was going to snap him in half.

"Humans mostly encountered my northern kin. The Orcs of the north tend to hold on to fat to keep warm, smaller eyes to keep the wind and ice out, and wide noses to sniff out food in a barren land." She reached up and poked her own nose; it did have a slight upturn, giving it a button-like look. "Me and mine, we're from the jungles south of Aquinas. No need for blubber for warmth; food is plentiful. Orcs are built for efficiency."

"I can see that," Dhali murmured, his ink-stained fingers tracing a scar across her lower back.

"You did well today, a good first battle." She turned to face him, and he had to step back to avoid being smacked by her ponderous chest. He had to consciously avoid licking his lips. "Go on, now wash my front."

Dhali opened and closed his mouth. He hesitated, unsure if she were being serious. But then again, why would she be joking? Was this a test? A test to ensure he was not simply some pervert?

She set her hand on her hip and raised an eyebrow. "Do you not *want* to wash me?"

He lowered his eyes, taking in her full majestic and savage beauty. Pale-green scars crisscrossed her body, and her muscles glistened from her powerful shoulders, toned arms, and stomach, all the way down her abdomen to the cut oblique muscles. He swallowed as his eyes came to the tuft of black hair just above the water and then her just-submerged pussy. Well, maybe this was a test or a trick and he would pay for it with his life, but godsdamn, he couldn't imagine anything more worth it.

He nodded and took a step forward, scooping to gather water in his hands, and rubbed her stomach. He could feel the muscles tense and relax under his fingers. Without looking up at her face, he traced the lines of her abs up before spreading his hands flat and running them under and then over her breasts.

He couldn't believe the difference between her hard stomach and soft breasts. He ran his thumb over her nipple, jostling the ring and drawing a sharp intake of breath of Korska. He looked up, meeting her eyes. There was no anger there, no sign of deception. He reached up with his right hand, his left hand continuing its exploration of her chest, reached around the back of her neck, and pulled her head down to kiss her. She didn't resist the pull, meeting his lips. He was kissing an Orc. The strangeness of the moment might have thrown him off, but her lips were softer than he could have ever imagined.

He let his left hand trail down her body, exploring the chiseled definition of her sides and hip before moving over her stomach and then down into the water. He felt her breath catch as his fingers found the folds of her sex and gently explored her.

She broke the kiss but kept her face against his, forehead to forehead. "Oh, maybe you aren't as shy as I thought. Here . . . " She reached down his arm. Her hand moved over his, guiding his fingers, dictating his rhythm. "There you go," she said, a smile on her lips.

He didn't mind the guidance, marveled at the feeling of her squeezing his fingers as she pushed him inside of her. The small whimper she made as he pushed and rubbed against and inside her surprised him and made him ache with need.

"You are a fast learner." She laughed, reaching down to slowly pull his hand away.

"You're a good teacher," he said.

"Mm, next lesson." She stepped away from him, moving to one of the large flat rocks on the banks of the river. He watched her go, staring at the way her hips and ass moved as she walked. It was almost too much for him, but when she turned to face him, sat on the stone, and spread her legs, giving him a full and perfect view of her pussy, he actually felt himself tremble.

He didn't need more invitation than that. He waded through the water towards her, grunting as his cock breached the water and the air moved across him. Reaching her, he fell to his knees and buried his face between her legs. He licked between the folds of her sex, where his fingers had been seconds ago, gently flicking his tongue across her clit.

"Oh, damn," he heard her say, then felt her hand push his shoulders up, forcing him away. "Some other time, but I want you inside me now."

He nodded, not trusting himself to speak. He rose to his feet and moved against her, laying his cock across her. He pulled back, using his hand to angle himself perfectly before once again pushing forward and slowly into her. She bit her lip, reaching down to wrap her hands around his hips and pull him in.

"No need to take your time. I am more than ready for

you." She held his hips for a second longer before releasing him and putting her hands under her to steady herself on the rock.

But he didn't need her to guide him or set a pace. He moved his hands over her thighs to her hips and then let them rest on her there as he fucked her. Each thrust brought a hiss of pleasure from Korska as he rocked his hips back only to ram into her again.

He leaned down over her but couldn't reach her face to kiss, so instead, he buried his face in her chest. He opened his mouth, sucking one of her light-green nipples into his mouth, flicking his tongue against her nipple and playing with the ivory ring there as he continued to pummel into her. He could feel her muscles constricting around his cock, squeezing him as her hips lifted from the rock. She arched her back, nearly suffocating him with her breasts. He couldn't hold on any longer. He put his hands down on either side of her, cumming hard as she bucked against him.

Even after he came, she writhed against him, the muscles of her pussy milking him for everything he was worth until he could no longer support his weight. He pulled away and stepped back, and she let out one last moan as he fell out of her. He moved and sat on the rock next to her.

Now that the sex was over, he was unsure what to do with himself. He reached out, rubbing a hand over Korska's stomach, still in awe of how incredibly sexy she looked. He would have never guessed he would be so aroused by an Orc.

"You felt good," Korska said, pulling herself to sitting and then sliding back into the water. "Very good."

"Thank you, you did too," he said, watching her. He was still breathless, and now, he was also cold. He rose from the rock and grabbed his robes. He considered going back and joining her again; getting dressed meant the moment was over. He decided against it, pulling the robes over his head and covering himself. After a moment, he glanced back at her, watching her move through the water. "What . . . " He paused, trying to figure out what he was trying to ask. "What does this mean?"

She raised an eyebrow. "It means nothing. If you are asking about relationships . . . " She shrugged. "I do not own you, and no one owns me. We are comrades in arms, and I believe that sharing physical closeness makes for better comrades, having that connection makes us fight harder for each other. Of course, your size and willingness to be a good student makes it all the better, but we are both free to live our lives."

Dhali nodded. He hadn't known what to expect, but if he were consigned to occasional mind-blowing sex with the powerful Korska for the duration of his time with the Host, well, he could imagine worse fates. "Korska, I think I'm going to return to camp," he said.

"Go on. I'm going to relax for a while. Until next time, Dhalius."

The thought of next time caused his heart to beat a bit faster, but he nodded and headed back west towards the camp.

MESSES

DHALI'S WALK BACK to camp made him realize he was much more sore than he had known. Still worth it. His mind was buzzing as he thought about his time with Korska, as though he were trying to cement the memory of the time in his brain. He had taken lovers before, here and there, but most of those had been clumsy attempts and rushed gropings behind a barn. The sort of things kids got into. Korska, on the other hand, was no kid, and there had been no confusion or hesitation.

Dhali entered the camp and walked towards the small tent that he would be calling his own for the time being. He noticed there seemed to be fewer glares thrown his way. Perhaps he had earned some small measure of respect during the battle. Or perhaps they were too tired to deal with the man in their midst. Either way, he reached his tent unmolested. He wondered when evening mess would be served; between the battle and his time at the river, he was feeling drained, battered, and ravenous. He threw back the flap to his tent and entered the darkness.

"About time," a voice said from the shadows, drawing a sharp yelp of surprise from Dhali.

"Ah, who?" Dhali asked. He reached for the lantern he had set on the trunk and fumbled for the matches when a sudden soft light filled the tent, emitting from a floating orb.

"Neela." Dhali exhaled, surprised to see the woman. She was dressed in a plain creme blouse and brown floor-length skirt as she sat on the edge of his cot.

"Yes." The shadows played off her sharp brown features, her green hair shimmering as the light hit it.

"I, what can I do for you?" he asked, figuring politeness would likely do him better than indignation.

"Disrobe. It's time for your physical exam," she said flatly. It would seem clinical if he didn't remember how his last exam had gone.

"What? Again? I just, uh, you examined me yesterday," he argued.

"I told you I am an Alarune. I need frequent watering," she said, raising an eyebrow. "And why are you protesting? I know you enjoyed it."

It took Dhali a moment to place the word. Alarunes were the product of strange magic, blood or semen from a hanged man soaking into the ground above a mandrake, giving life to creatures that were neither human nor plant but some strange mix of the two. They were supposed to be soulless and cruel. That might explain her flat affect.

"Uh, well, I'm not sure I'm up for . . . watering. I was just—" He paused, unsure if it were wise to admit what had happened with Korska. But on the other hand, she had seemed unconcerned. "I was just with Korska. I'm feeling bruised, and empty."

Her eyebrows shot up in surprise. "With Korska? You mean . . . *with* her." She rose from the cot. "Disrobe." She repeated her earlier command.

Dhalius, at a loss, pulled the robe over his head. "I'm just not sure I would be able to—" He stopped as he felt her hand, so much smaller and gentler than Korska's had been, touch the base of his cock.

"Then you are lucky I am here," she said as gentle cooling spread from her touch and through his body. He could feel the weariness and aches evaporating. "See, isn't that better?" she asked, wrapping her small fingers around the girth of his shaft, using both hands to fully encircle it. He could feel himself getting hard again, the exhaustion of the day having left him.

She paused. "You didn't wash after your time with her, did you?" Her tone was accusatory, but there was a devious glint in her eyes.

"Well, I had just bathed before she came, so . . . "

"So her essence is still on you. I want to taste it." Before he could react, she dropped to her knees in front of him and ran her tongue from the base of his cock all the way down to the tip. "A delicious combination." She looked up at him, her eyes glowing in the gloom, he realized.

She didn't give him a chance to respond as she dipped her head down and enveloped the head of his manhood in her mouth, using her hands to guide more and more of him down her throat. Dhalius caught himself on the trunk, holding himself steady as the Alarune began bobbing her head, her tongue swishing over him.

"Gods," he whispered, watching her.

One of her hands rubbed up his stomach, the other reaching around to cup his ass as she continued to swallow him. She let out a moan, which reverberated through the flesh of his cock, making him shudder from pleasure.

Suddenly, she pulled back, a thick strand of saliva stretching between her lips and his glistening flesh. "Stop being so passive," she commanded, pushing his dick out of the way and sucking his balls into her mouth.

He almost shouted at the sudden and intense sensation of her tongue tracing over the incredibly sensitive skin. She let his balls fall out of her mouth and rubbed her face against them and then his cock.

"What?" he gasped, trying to catch his breath. "What do you mean?"

She grabbed his shaft, continuing to rub her face along its length. "You look at me, and you see a frail healer. I am no girl to be treated with gently. I want every inch of you down my throat. You fucked Korska; now fuck my face!" She wasted no time, pulling back and sitting on her heels as she opened her mouth wide and looked at him expectantly.

Dhali used his hand to guide himself into Neela's waiting mouth before dropping his hands to either side of her head, curling his fingers through her hair. He wasn't sure what to do but figured he had to take her at her word and began thrusting, gently at first, just a few inches. He was still worried about hurting her. But as he entered her mouth, she swirled the top of her tongue along the underside of his cock, tracing the veins. She reached between his legs, cupping his ass with her dainty hands, and pushed his hips forward hard, ramming him down her throat. He gasped as her nose hit his stomach. Her moan reverberated through him, pulling forth his own groan of pleasure.

Her signal and guidance were clear. He cupped her head in his hands to keep her in place and began to thrust into her mouth, pulling back before once again sliding in to the very base. The tightness of her throat squeezed him, and her hands dropped to his thighs so she could steady herself against his movements.

He looked down at her, his fingers curling to run through her green hair and gently scratch her scalp. She met his gaze and widened her mouth to allow her tongue to snake out and lick at his balls as he pushed as deep as he could. The sight was almost too much for him.

"Neela—" he croaked to warn her, pulling back, but she snaked her arms back to his ass and shoved him violently into her. His cock slid down her throat as he came with such force it made him nearly double over, hugging her head to his chest. His hips bucked, pressing her face into him as he felt his balls spasm, her throat muscles working to massage every last drop of cum from him.

Finally, he released her and fell back. The sensation caused by sliding out of her throat and the light graze of her teeth against his skin as he did drew another shuddered groan from him. He collapsed against his trunk and watched as she wiped her mouth on her sleeve, cleaning herself of the mix of saliva and semen that had leaked out. She nodded in apparent self-satisfaction and stood.

"That was incredible." Dhali panted.

"It was enjoyable, I agree," Neela said, the mask of bored indifference slipping over her features once again. "Less to clean too, less waste. Now it's your turn to eat."

"Oh!" Dhali nodded. He was spent but wouldn't turn her down by any means. He licked his lips and rose onto his knees.

She gave him an odd look. "Not me. It's suppertime in the camp."

"Oh," he said, a little disappointed, but rose and grabbed his robes. He spoke as he pulled them over his head. "I know you are here to, uh, I suppose feed, but I enjoy your—" But as his head cleared the robe, he found himself alone in the tent. More sore now than he had been before, he shrugged and headed out into camp to get his food.

He endured the dirty looks and snide comments as he made his way through camp to the commons area, though he noticed there were fewer this evening than there had been in the morning. Perhaps his performance in the battle had earned him enough grace to make it through the next stretch until Captain Lakista replaced him. He stood in line, keeping his eyes turned downward. He wanted to look around. Ten-Tulips' words echoed in his mind about how this was such an opportunity to get to know such a diverse group of cultures and tactics. He knew if he appeared like a farm boy at a livestock show, he would likely be put to the sword before he could explain himself.

Once he had a plate of hardtack, wild game brought in by the rangers, and boiled vegetables gifted from the farmers of Zachman's Crossing, he looked up to try to find an empty, or at least emptier, table to sit at. Those who saw him looking closed ranks. He was about to head back to his tent to eat when a voice cut through the din.

"Dhalius, come, join us!" Korska called, standing up to make herself *even* more visible.

Relieved, he hurried through the crowd and approached the table. Korska, seeing he had found his way, sat back down and nodded her head at an empty seat on the bench across from her, between two other warriors. They didn't look terribly pleased but made no move to block him.

"Thank you, Korska," he said, sitting and setting his tray down.

"Dhalius, this is my squad. Henrietta Vanberg." She gestured to a Dwarven woman who's tattooed knuckles were wrapped around a shank bone.

She grunted an acknowledgement. "Call me Henri," she said around a mouthful.

Dhali had met plenty of Dwarves in his time at the Academy, and she seemed on par with those he knew, braided honey-colored hair, deep blue eyes, and muscles that looked like corded steel. She had a solid hourglass figure and wore her scale mail like a second skin.

"Gisla NoNachtin."

He didn't know what Gisla was, but her bronze skin shimmered, her hair glowed like embers, and she gave off waves of heat as she glanced at him, then back to her plate. She was almost ethereal to behold, like the flame of a candle had come to life and decided to inhabit a statue of a human goddess to imitate humanity.

"And Tawna Jacks," Korska finished, gesturing to the woman sitting to his left.

Tawna was a Draconid, something he had never come face-to-face with before. Humanoids said to have been created as servants for dragons, they were known as fierce warriors with little humor or patience, and with a penchant for cannibalizing other races. He watched her tear into her meat, and swallowed. She had bright green and blue scales, and golden eyes with snakelike slits for pupils.

"A pleasure to meet you all, and Dhali will suffice—"

"Your magic," Tawna interrupted him, swallowing her meat. "What was it? I've not seen the likes before."

"Aye, it was weird," Henrietta agreed.

"Ye tink all magic is weird," Gisla scoffed.

"Mebbe because our word for magic is wyrd," Henrietta returned.

"Maybe let the mage answer?" Korska asked as she dug into her food.

Dhalius gave her a grateful smile. "Well, we're called scribes, but the official name is Atramentomancer, which . . . admittedly, is a mouthful. We use enchanted inks to enact our magic and will. It's not the most popular school because it relies on reagents more than most spellwork, and it's less flashy than other schools—"

"Looked plenty flashy to me!" Henrietta laughed, the other joined in, and Dhali felt himself relaxing more among the squad. He didn't mention that his particular school was also considered more difficult to master, nor it's sinister reputation amongst students as a favorite of more darkly inclined wizards.

"Fair," he agreed. "But we are also limited. Once we run out of ink, well, I am grateful that you all had our backs out there. Without your blades and strength, I would be resting comfortably in the belly of the undead now."

Now that the tension had been broken, the squad spoke amongst themselves with an easy familiarity that Dhalius tried to keep up with. He thought back on Korska's philosophy of physical intimacy in camaraderie and wondered if that was why they were all so comfortable with each other. He shook the thoughts away as being none of his business but was relieved he was being allowed to join them.

"Settle a bet, Dhali," Henri said, gesturing with her shank bone. "I say the reason human men sport no good beard is because yer also descended from lizards. Tawna thinks it's because ye shave it all off fer being more streamlined, smoother."

Dhalius opened and closed his mouth several times, trying to wrap his mind around the insanity of either statement. Korska leaned forward, her chin resting on the back of her hands, an amused grin on her face. He was struck again at how beautiful her strength and features were. "There are many men with full beards, Henri—"

"Not good ones!" she argued.

"Well, be that as it may, I shave—" he continued

"Hah!" Tawna exclaimed.

"But not to be more . . . streamlined, whatever that means. I just think I look better without a—"

"You look even *worse* with a beard?" Gisla gasped, but a moment later burst into laughter, revealing that she was—hopefully—just teasing.

Dhalius was about to defend himself when he felt a hand fall on his shoulder. Looking up, he met the eyes of a severe-looking human woman. "Captain Lakista requests your presence."

"I . . . " The color drained from Dhalius's face, and he looked around at the women at the table. "Have I done something to—"

"Just gather your things and attend. We have a prisoner in need of your . . . attention."

PRISONER TAKEN

DHALIUS FOLLOWED THE severe woman back through the camp to a circle of tents that was fenced off. There, strapped to a stake, was a half-nude man covered in bruises and cuts. He wore a terrifying smile that grew as he saw Dhalius approach. Nearby, Lakista stood, her face a grim, angry shadow. Next to her stood a gangly woman, all jutting limbs with gnarled blue skin stretched over her bones, reminding Dhali of a worn scarecrow. The curved tusks that jutted from her lips made her identifiable as a Troll, though he had never seen one in person. Her arms were covered in blood, and she stood next to a tray of gory instruments. Ten-Tulips was also there, still in her baggy robes. She offered Dhali a tight-lipped smile as he approached.

"Mage," Lakista barked. "We need information from this"—her lips curled in disgust—"man. You are to extract it."

"Captain, I—I'm no torturer. I'm certainly not skilled as someone like her." He bowed to the Troll woman, assuming she was either a medic or a skilled interrogator. "Nor do I have the tools that Mistress Ten-Tulips has at her disposal."

"Aw, let the lad be." The bloodied man cackled from his perch. "He's squeamish. We can keep playing, Captain."

Lakista ignored him. "I am giving you a direct order, mage."

"Yes, I know that." He stepped forward and whispered.

"But I do not know *why* you are asking me to handle this. I've no training in torture or interrogation."

"Presumably, you have training in magic?" she asked, sneering at him.

"Yes, Captain," he answered, turning red.

"Well, somehow, this maggot has used magic to protect himself. Ten-Tulips is unable to dispel it, Ashakat is at a loss, so I called for my bloody *mage*." She hissed the last part.

"I understand, Captain, but I feel very uncomfortable in this role. It is not something I—"

She grabbed his arm and yanked him around violently, almost wrenching the limb from the socket, nearly pushing him to the ground, and towered above him, her eyes blazing in rage. "You listen well, boy. These necromancer scum have absconded with my soldiers, my sisters, my women. They took them, and do you *know* what men do with female prisoners? Do you know what necromancers do once they are done with the living?" Her fingers dug into his flesh through the robe painfully.

"Yes, Captain," he whispered hoarsely.

"So, you *will* find out where they have taken them. And then *you* will lead a team to retrieve them. *Do* you understand me?" she snarled.

"Perfectly, Captain," he agreed. She released him and he stumbled, but Ten-Tulips caught him before he landed on his ass and helped him rise.

"Oooh, she's scary," the prisoner sang in a lilting falsetto. "Whatever will I—"

"No," Dhalius said softly, his voice deadpan. "She isn't. But I am." He approached the man. "I said I was uncomfortable with hurting a prisoner, not that I couldn't, not that I was . . . incapable." He stopped a few inches short of the prisoner, looking up to where the man was tied. "See, I know your secret, not so much a secret, just something that those who haven't studied the arcane arts wouldn't know. But I do. I did study them. I even studied necromancy. You have to know what it is to hunt it, you see." He paused.

"I know your kind deaden your skin, an effort to be more like your minions, more like the things you so admire. You're insensate to all external stimulus, making it impossible to hurt you, and well, you don't fear death because you worship it. So if my friend here let loose, you would let go and die, a win for you, and our friends would be lost."

The man's maniacal smile widened. "Oh, you've become quite talkative."

"Shh," Dhalius said, raising a finger to the man's lips. "You are almost dead already, except . . . for . . . here." He reached up with his other hand and tapped his own skull. "Your mind. The only thing you actually care about. The only thing more sacred than power."

The man's smile dropped.

Dhalius brought his finger away from the man's lips and held it in front of his nose. "And I don't need much to get at it, not much at all. They could cut all day and never scare you. All I need is one drop." The ink stain on his index finger began to peel away, jittering and spasming until a small spider made of ink danced on his finger tip. "Shall we begin?"

The spider leapt from Dhalius's finger and quickly climbed up the bound man's nose. His eyes went wide, and seconds later, his screams filled the air. Dhalius remained motionless, his eyes thrumming with a violet light as he concentrated on the spell. He truly did not like doing this, he didn't enjoy the more cruel applications of the power of Scribes, but he would go to any means to retrieve the women of the Host and bring them back safely.

Within minutes, the man had been reduced to tears, sobbing and begging for Dhali to stop. Dhali didn't. He stripped the man of his knowledge, figuratively and literally. He would let words spill from the man's mouth, and then he would destroy another bit of the man's mind.

His ink-crafted arachnid devoured his brain bit by bit until he was effectively lobotomized. Finished, Dhali let his hand drop to his side.

He had gotten less information than he would have liked. He learned it was likely that the force they had fought this morning was merely an exploratory splinter group. The master of the cult, one who had risen to power recently, and their army was still to come. But mostly, he now knew where the captives would probably have been taken, a small ruin just a few kilometers southwest of where they had done battle, deep within the forest.

For several minutes, all of them were silent, listening to the soft mindless groan of the former necromancer. Finally, Lakista spoke.

"Good job, mage. Go get what you need, join with Tzacha on the northern edge of the camp. You know your target." With that, she turned and walked off.

Ashakat, the Troll, eyed him up and down and smirked. "Good to know you have use," she grunted before gathering her tools and following after the captain.

Ten-Tulips put her hand on Dhalius's hand, looking up at him with a worried expression. "Are you okay?"

He smiled down at her. "Yeah," he lied. He wrapped his fingers around her much smaller hand and gave it a squeeze. "Thank you." He released her and frowned. "You said you think you could make ink for me?"

"Ink? Oh! Yes, I think so, If you—"

"Come by my tent in a few minutes; I'll give you all the details and instructions I have. Thank you again, Ten." He spared one last glance at the man, who drooled incoherently, now bound for no reason but to keep him upright, and walked away.

In his tent, Dhalius wrote a quick list on a spare scrap of parchment for Ten regarding the items needed to make the ink. He *could* make it himself, or buy regular ink and then find a shop or scavenge the reagents needed to complete it. But it would be much faster and more potent if an actual alchemist crafted the ink for him to enchant. He fastened his spell book to his waist, nervous about how few usable pages remained, and stepped out of the tent.

Seeing Ten, he hurried to her and handed the list over. "Thank you again!" he shouted as he hurried past her, knowing that if he let her, she would suck him into a conversation that made him late to meet up with the whoever it was waiting for him to "lead" the rescue. A few minutes later, he arrived at the edge of the camp. He saw a group of Elves and a Dryad. They looked impatient and sported dark clothes and bows—the rescue party, he assumed. He hurried over to them.

One of the Elves looked him up and down, sneering. "Male."

He wondered if it was the same woman as before. To his human eyes, each of the Elves could be close sisters. Blond, ice-blue eyes, pale skin, and, most of all, an expression of utter disgust and disdain.

"Sorry, I had to go gather my belongings," he explained. "And make sure I had rea—"

"I don't care," the Elf cut him off. "Tzacha will be going with you. She is leading this rescue; you are there to ensure she can counter their magic. Make sure you do not get in her way."

"Wait, just two of us? Going into an enemy camp?" He gaped at her. "I assumed—"

"You assumed it would be smarter to send an entire platoon to make noise and ensure they kill their captives? That does seem like something you would assume," she said dismissively.

"This is not an attack. It is a rescue. We want to draw little attention and escape with our sisters and as much intelligence as we can." This was said by the only non-Elf in the group. The Dryad stepped forward. Her green eyes held none of the animosity of the Elves'. "I am Tzacha. You are the mage, Darius?" She offered her hand.

Relieved, he took it. "Dhalius, or Dhali. I am as ready as I can be." He decided to ignore the Elves for now—they didn't like him; they didn't have to like him. He would focus on the courteous Dryad instead.

"Then let's off." She turned and began moving at a light jog, heading into the woods.

He took a deep breath and followed after, hoping she would remember that he did not have a Dryad's endurance.

As he caught up to her, she glanced over at him from under long, dark lashes. She was a beautiful creature whose natural beauty mirrored that of the forest. They traveled in silence for several minutes, entering into the forest and making their way through the underbrush. She navigated the tricky terrain easily and gracefully. It was a wonder humans had survived in this world full of creatures and species that were so much better suited for it than them. He had heard stories of Dryads before. Of Nymphs and Fauns, nature spirits who delighted in splendid orgies and wanton acts under the full moons. He wondered if those stories held any water. Though seeing one in action now, it was hard to imagine her in such a setting.

"You are wondering if I want to have sex with you," she said suddenly.

"What?" he asked, startled. "No, I wasn't—"

"Because I am a Nymph," she finished. "Humans have certain notions about us. It is okay. It is natural to be curious, but we must focus on the task at hand."

"Yes, of course," he said, feeling like he was being dragged along behind her in this conversation, the same way he was being forced to keep pace physically.

"And, yes. I do wish to have sex with you. Neela says you have a very serviceable phallus. But it is not time for that. Once we rescue our sisters and are safely back at camp, perhaps we can find time, if you survive."

Dhalius didn't answer right away. He was torn between the extreme embarrassment of the conversation and the secret pride at knowing he had been discussed favorably.

"Ah, I made you uncomfortable. I forget that humans, particularly males, are somewhat shy about this topic." She chuckled.

"Yes," he agreed. "But also, it is such a strange juxtaposition. Most of the Defiant Host acts as if I am a leper; they look like they want to slit my throat and leave me on the side of the road. A precious few are friendly. And then there's those like Neela and . . . " He paused, not feeling comfortable discussing Korska without permission. "Who want to fuck."

"You are new. And you are different than almost every other member of the Host. You have much to prove. But if and when you do, you will find those differences matter less and less. Give respect, show courage, show worth, and all other things float away. Oh, and humility, show proper humility; this will go a long way."

"Thank you, Tzacha," he said.

"You are welcome, Dhalian," she said, getting his name wrong again, but with a smile that was as warm as the sun that had already begun dipping low over the horizon.

They fell back into silence as they continued on, and while the darkness made them slow so Dhali didn't trip over himself, they continued moving through the night. After hours of their trekking through the forest, they were nearing the necromancer's base of operations, at least according to their captive. Dhali was fairly certain the man had been telling the truth. He had devoured his ability to lie fairly early in the process. But Dhalius was exhausted. He had fought in a battle in the morning, had two intimate encounters, tortured a man, and now, nearly twenty hours later without rest, was engaged in a rescue mission. He prayed when this was done, he would finally be allowed to rest.

He was about to suggest they take a moment to recover their stamina when something detached from the tree beside him and wrapped around his throat. A rotting hand clamped over his mouth, and he was dragged off his feet.

Tzacha, ahead of him, whipped around at the sound of struggling, a bow suddenly in her hands.

"Lower the weapon, little bitch, or I'll empty your friend's guts in the dirt." The voice was cruel and gruff.

A torch was lit, blinding Dhalius for a moment, but he could just make out the shadows of men. They were surrounded. As his eyes adjusted, he saw Tzacha, her face drawn into an angry scowl. Her arrow was notched and ready to fly, directly at *him*. He knew what she was thinking. If she killed him, she could probably skewer his throat and kill the man holding him and then escape. No leverage, no worries. He met her eyes and nodded.

She drew back, and then, with a growl of frustration, lowered her bow. Dhalius didn't have time to wonder why she didn't follow through, as a moment later, something heavy and hard crashed into his skull and the world went dark.

TAKEN PRISONER

D HALIUS SLOWLY OPENED one eye and then another. He was hanging from manacles attached to a moldering stone wall in a room that could only truly be described as dank. The musty smell of fungal rot and decay filled his nostrils. As the room itself swam into focus, he could see he was not alone. On the wall across from him, Tzacha hung in manacles similar to his own. She looked worse for the wear, her left eye swollen shut, her lip busted. She had obviously fought to not be taken. He looked around slowly, hissing in pain as he moved.

"Ah, the boy awakens!" The voice boomed and sent a spike of pain through Dhali. "Welcome, boy."

The speaker was a large, intimidating man. The shadows hid most of the details from Dhalius, but he looked like a brigand to him.

"Try to find his name before you kill him," a bored voice said from the corner.

Dhalius looked up to see a frail man, quill in hand, taking notes next to a candle, his hands stained with ink. Cults and their records, scholars of dark lore and murder.

"Ah, well, we don't have to kill this one; he's a mage. A Scribe! He's like to be one of us." The large man approached him and used one giant hand to turn Dhalius's head from left to right, inspecting him. "Just because he runs with the whores and bitches don't make him one." He grinned, revealing half-rotted teeth and breath that could knock out a horse.

"That won't happen," Dhalius muttered.

"Ah, don't be so negative." He looked over at Tzacha. "Or maybe you ain't negative. Is that your woman, then? Is that the issue?" He took a few steps away from Dhalius. "I don't mind sharing, boy." He chuckled as he reached out to push Tzacha's hair out her eyes. "After all, we have the girls in the other room, plenty to go—"

"Don't you fucking touch her," Dhalius growled.

"My gods, I touched a nerve. So she *is* your woman." He laughed and patted Tzacha's cheek. "Oh, I'm going to do more than touch her. I'm going to have her, again and again." He watched Dhalius for his reaction.

"Do you need to antagonize him, Barkus?" the scholar asked.

"Absolutely. Don't worry, he's impotent; we took his book. Without his precious ink, he's powerless." The man laughed again. "And soon, the whole world will be powerless. You see, mage, we found what we needed. We have the staff."

"The staff?" Dhalius asked. He closed his eyes and focused his will on his fingers, pulling the ink into a long pin.

Barkus gestured to a gnarled haft of wood a little less than a meter in length in the corner of the room. Even in the shadows, it seemed to shimmer, laced with veins of intricate luminous opal. "St. Viscu's Staff of the Anchorite, it is magnificent, and when Goana arrives—"

"Goana!" Tzacha gasped.

"Oh yes. You are familiar with our Mistress, aren't you?" Barkus said, turning back to her. "She used to run with you whores, didn't she? Sacrificed a lot of you in Fralt."

"You're being rather free with your words, Barkus," the scholar chided.

"Gods, shut up!" the man roared. "They're both dead. I'll slit the mage's throat, and I'll have this woman until she breaks."

"You won't lay another finger on her," Dhalius called.

"Godsdamnit, you're insistent, like a little brother. She isn't your woman, is she? You ain't got a woman at all, do you?" He chuckled and moved towards Dhalius again, continuing his ping-ponging between the two. "You know what's the best part of working for necromancers? I can play with her till she breaks, and then raise her and keep playing."

"You won't—"

"I will! Why do you object to a woman's natural use? Are you a eunuch?" He used his sword to lift Dhalius's robe. "Holy fuck, look at this, Grandil, nearly to his damn knees! All right, not a eunuch, but ain't worth much of anything if you aren't using it."

"I have never had issues with women, Barkus," Dhalius said. "I never needed to resort to force or threats; they've liked me without it."

"Oh, look at you all high and mighty now." Barkus laughed. "I like it rough."

"Rough is fine; you like it unwilling. That doesn't make you a man; it makes you a pathetic, disgusting worm." He spat the words and let go of the manacles he had freed himself from minutes ago using his ink-formed pick. As he fell, he brought his fist down and landed a solid punch. When he hit the ground, he immediately kicked out as hard as he could against Barkus's knee. It didn't take much. With a terrible crunch, the man's knee bent backwards, and he fell to the ground screaming.

"How the hell did you get free?" Grandil shrieked, pulling out a curved dagger and waving it at Dhalius.

Dhalius didn't answer. He raised his hand, and his eyes blazed with arcane light.

"You can't do shit without your ink book. You are powerless!"

Dhali closed his fist, and the scholar dropped to the floor as the ink stains on his fingers suddenly constricted, crushing his hands.

"No." Dhalius said, just over the sound of the two men's mewlings. "It's just more difficult. We can work with any ink." He picked up Barkus's sword and walked towards the scholar. "It's less potent, less . . . reactive. But it still works; it's still more than enough to deal with you." He kicked the man onto his back and, with a simple thrust, pushed the sword through the man's screaming mouth and into the stone floor beneath him.

With a gesture, he pulled the ink from the scribe's hands, forming solid ink knuckle dusters around his fingers. "You said you like it rough?" he called as he stalked towards Barkus.

"You keep away, you stay away from me, you freak," Barkus cried, trying to crawl away.

"Not so fun when you're the unwilling one?" Dhalius asked. He reached down and turned Barkus onto his back and straddled him. "Let's find out."

Minutes later, Dhalius lifted himself up from the corpse and let his ink-formed weapons dissolve. He reached down and pulled the keys dangling from Barkus's belt and rushed to Tzacha.

She watched him cautiously. "You are a dangerous man," she whispered hoarsely.

"Only to our enemies," he answered as he reached up to free her.

As she fell, she caught his shoulders, using him to steady herself. She pressed herself against him as she regained her composure. He breathed slowly, trying to calm his own heartbeat and overcome the adrenaline rush.

"We have to get out of here before more—"

"You go, take the staff. I'm going to look for the others," he interrupted her.

"No, we can look together. It's dangerous," she protested.

"Tzacha, you have to get the staff back to Lakista. I

don't know exactly what it is, but I can feel its power from here. And you have to warn them about Goana. I don't know who—"

When he said the name, Tzacha's eyes narrowed in furious hate. She looked over at the staff and back to him, pulling herself up and away from him, steadied by her rage. Still she hesitated. "I don't like leaving you on your own."

"You were caught because I was stumbling and falling. If not for me, you could have gotten in here, freed them, and been back by now, unharmed," he said firmly. "Going on your own gives us the greatest chance of you getting back to the Host. That is the most important thing in all the world right now." He walked back to the body of the scholar to retrieve the sword. "Now take the staff and get out of here. I'll find any survivors, and we'll do our best to make our way back to camp." He gave her one final nod and headed through the doorway.

According to his interrogation, those that had taken captives had been a small group, just enough to transport and watch over the captives while the main force had rejoined the House of the Rotting Eaves main camp, somewhere in the swamps even further south than Zachman's Crossing. He didn't have exact numbers because the prisoner hadn't had them, but from his own knowledge and guesswork, he would estimate that other than Barkus and the scholar, there was likely just one necromancer and its minions remaining.

Death cults did not suffer the presence of the living lightly. They had unending numbers of undead servants, but if you killed their masters, then the whole force could be destroyed easily. Still, the zombies would be a terrifying threat if they spotted him; he would be overwhelmed. But if Dhali had to guess—and he dare not use his magic to confirm lest he reveal himself to his enemies—he would think the dead were outside, guarding the exterior of the ruins. Barkus had been too assured of himself, too cocky that no one was coming to save them.

Luckily for Dhalius, the ruins weren't so large as to be labyrinthine. Still, it was slow going. For an hour or longer, he followed the hallways through the crumbling fortress, his hand against the wall to guide him in the near total darkness, taking his time to not trigger any traps or knock over any debris to give his location away. One small mistake, one misstep, and he could have a flesh-eating horde rushing in to devour him. After the long minutes of exploring the area, he saw the flickering of a torch ahead of him. He stalked forward, readying his sword as he moved carefully across the threshold of the large room.

A black-robed figure stood in the center of the room, his back turned to Dhalius. Around him, five zombies milled mindlessly, their minds incapable of understanding that Dhalius was a threat without direct orders from their master. On the opposite side of the room, four women, battered and bruised, were bound together with thick ropes. He couldn't be sure, but they all seemed fully dressed, unmolested.

A small blessing when dealing with necromancers, the same spells that deadened their flesh also made them impotent, incapable of performing even if they did indeed feel lust—which Dhali wouldn't put money on. He crept up behind the rival mage as silently as he was able, counting on the groans and shuffling of the damned to hide his movements. Luckily for him, the cultist's attention was focused on the captives and not on the world around him. He, like so many magic-users, put total stock in their powers, assuming it could solve every problem.

If Dhalius used magic, it would likely draw the attention of the cultist, and with that, every shambling horror in the vicinity. However, Dhalius held not a spellbook but the cold iron of a sword. He stepped up behind the oblivious necromancer and rammed the blade through his back, angled so it might slip through ribs and puncture the heart, and hopefully a lung as well.

"The Defiant Host sends its greetings," he hissed

through clenched teeth, then kicked the man's body off the blade. Dhalius raised the blade, ready for the onslaught of rotting nails and broken teeth, but all around him, the undead fell, their animating force fleeing their bodies as quickly as the life left that of their master.

"Thank the gods," Dhalius whispered and hurried forward to cut through the ropes that bound the women.

"You're the mage," one whispered hoarsely.

"That I am," he answered.

"There are more of them, a big man," said another, a lizard-folk if he was not mistaken. "He wanted to—"

"Dead," Dhalius said, meeting her eyes. "The cultist, the bruiser, and the scholar are dead. Are there any more? Anyone else other than the dead?" he asked as he finished freeing them.

Slowly, they rose, rubbing their arms and stretching. One woman couldn't rise on her own, her leg obviously broken. Dhalius knelt beside her and lifted her on his shoulder so she could use him as a crutch.

"None that we saw," answered a massive woman with curved horns and hooves, whose arms were as thick as his thighs. After answering, she began picking up weapons dropped by the undead as they fell.

"Good, great. I sent Tzacha ahead . . . she's on her way back to camp. But we should make our way out. I don't think there are any more of them here, but there will be. They said, the big one said that someone named Goana was leading them."

The woman he was propping up stiffened, and all four women stared at him.

"Goana?" one asked.

"Yes," he affirmed.

The women looked between themselves, a steely angry resolve hardening in their eyes. "Let's go," the big woman with horns said—Dhalius wondered if she was part minotaur. He nodded, and the group began the work of making their way out of the ruins and through the forest.

But they were in bad shape. All of them, Dhali included, had been beaten and sleep deprived. They were spent and injured, not to mention, Dhalius was the only one who had eaten anything in the last twenty-four hours. The group staggered on, taking turns supporting their hobbled friend. They did not speak as they marched through the darkness and the sun began to rise over the hills to the east. Dhalius wasn't sure he was capable of taking too many more steps when the most beautiful sight he had ever seen in his life greeted them. As they broke the edge of the forest, five Elvish rangers were making their way across the horizon.

"Palaas!" the Minotauress—her name was Jaxsi and she was one of the lieutenants of the Host, he had discovered—called, waving to catch their attention. "The gods are good. We are rescued."

Dhalius nodded, finding himself unable to speak. Between the marching, beating, and casting, he was spent. He had pushed his body further than it could go naturally and then again pushed it further than he could in arcane measures. He smiled back at her and changed direction so they could intercept the Elves.

HEALING TOUCH

T HE ELVES ESCORTED the five of them back to camp and then straight towards the medical tent. However, Palaas stopped Dhalius with a hand on his chest before he could enter. "Not you."

"I . . . I'm injured too," he argued weakly.

"This is a medical tent for women. They need not a *man* in their midst," she stated bluntly. "Go to your own tent, wait for treatment there."

He noticed that all eyes were on him, but no one spoke up to defend or argue on his behalf. And he certainly didn't have the strength to argue with her.

"Understood," he said curtly and limped through the camp back to his tent.

He had hoped he would see friendly faces on his way, anyone he could ask for a hand or to help him get some water. The rangers had given them water and food on their march back, but it had been travel rations and did nothing to blunt the heady need for comfort. A bucket of water and a rag would be a godsend too, to wipe away the blood and grime. But no luck there. He had to assume they were all busy with their own duties.

Reaching his tent, he slipped in and sat on the edge of his cot. He was about to lie down when the flap of his tent opened. He glanced up hoping it would be Neela's soothing healing or Ten with some potion that would dissolve his aches. Instead, Captain Lakista stood in full armor scowling down at him. She held the staff in her hand.

"No time to rest, mage. Tzacha said you claimed this staff was important and that they serve—"

"Goana," he finished for her. "Captain, I swear on my life and my balls that you, Tzacha, and the others know everything I do. I don't know who this Goana is other than it's someone known to all of you, someone you seem to hate, and the staff . . . " He gestured at it and shrugged. "All I know is it is powerful, some magical relic, but without study and time, I couldn't tell you anything else."

"Then it sounds like you should get to work." She thrust the staff toward him.

He looked at it and then at her. "Would you treat *any* woman under your command this way? Marched, battered, bruised, and offered no succor, healing, or mercy?"

"You are not a woman," she hissed.

"No, but I *am* under your command," he shot back.

She frowned, her scowl deepening and then falling away entirely to a weary expression.

"No. I wouldn't. I wouldn't be so unkind, and I shouldn't be." She straightened up and cleared her throat. "You did commendable work. Marched, fought, aided in interrogation, led a successful rescue mission, and came back with important intelligence. Understand, mage, that Goana is the reason you are here. She betrayed the Host and killed a great many of us, some . . . ritual to appease the dark god she served in secret. If this staff is important to her, it is important to us. I don't know how much time we have before her army marches, or how we are meant to face her as is. The answer to that question may well be in this staff, and you are our only battle mage. You may be the only person who can answer that for us in time." She offered him the staff again.

This time, he took it. "I can't do anything until I rest, Captain. I am beyond exhausted."

She nodded, looking down at him, maybe not with compassion but at least with understanding. "Get some rest. I will send someone with food and water, but you are excused from all other duties until we know what this staff is.”

“And . . . if I could get a bucket of water and a rag, something to clean myself, else I’ll need to head to the river and—”

“I’ll have them bring it.” She cut him off. She turned to leave and paused in the open tent flap. “Good work, mage. I am grateful for what you did.” And with those words, which he knew had to physically hurt her to say, she left.

True to her word, his tent flap opened once more not ten minutes later, and Korska stepped in carrying a bucket and a tray of food—bread, meats, some fruit, and even a bit of cheese.

“Oh thank the gods,” he gasped, seeing the food.

“Good to see you too, Dhali.” Korska smirked.

“Sorry, I’m famished.”

“I imagine. I told off Captain Lakista after you left. Sending you without one of the squad was a rash decision; one of us should have been with you. Now get out of those filthy robes.”

“Oh I’m in no shape,” he protested.

“I know,” she said patiently. “But you washed me, so let me return the favor.” She set the tray on his trunk and helped him out of his robes. “You focus on eating.”

He was constantly surprised by Korska. She was strength and brutality incarnate on the battlefield, and he would have bet his life that she was rough and tumble in all aspects of her humors, had he been asked an hour ago. He sat on the stool in his tent and closed his eyes as Korska dipped a rag into the water and began gently rubbing his back. Her gentleness and the juxtaposition of such a docile act against the strength of her form and the scars that crisscrossed her skin made her the very definition of beauty in his mind. He was relieved that his body was too exhausted to react to her company.

He ate slowly, careful not to make himself sick, as the

Orc gently scrubbed him clean. She hummed as she did so. He did not know the song, but it was deep and resonate, and he could feel the thrum in his bones.

"What is that song?" he asked between bites of an apple.

"Just an old Orcish hunting song. My Pa would sing it as he readied for a raid or a hunt. It is meant to soothe the soul and bring one into alignment with the world."

"I like it," he said as her hand traced circles around his chest and ran across his stomach.

She washed his legs, thighs, and cock with neither the clumsy advances of a teenage lover nor the cold detachment of a warfield nurse. Now, his body couldn't help but stiffen under her attention.

"You should tell your cock that you're not up for a tumble," she teased.

"Sorry," he said, blushing lightly.

"Don't be. I am flattered it remembers me." She chuckled throatily and kissed the back of his neck. Her hands moved away from him, leaving him aching in a different way. "But we'll have time to enjoy that when you are healed." She stood, reached over, and grabbed his dirtied robes, tossing them into the bucket of now dirty, bloody water. "I'll add these to our squads' clothes for launder. I assume you have something else you can wear."

"Yes. I do. Thank you, Korska." He nodded.

She smiled and let her eyes linger on his erection, her pink tongue flicking out to lick her lips. "Get better quickly. Captain Lakista has formally assigned you to my squad, so that *is* a command," she said, then grabbed the now empty tray and made her way from the tent.

Dhalius glanced down at his erection, which was already beginning to flag. He opened his trunk and pulled out a fresh robe, but instead of putting it on, he wrapped it around himself like a blanket, fell into his cot, and promptly fell asleep.

When he woke up, Dhalius felt amazingly refreshed. He never would have believed that he had spent the previous day and a half marching through hell. He rose and stretched, quickly pulling his robes over his head and dressing. He intended to go out into the camp to get breakfast before he started his work but noticed a cloth-covered tray on his trunk and a fresh bucket of water next to the flap. Lifting the cloth revealed a plate of bread and sliced fruit, as well as several large flasks filled with shimmering purple, blue, and red inks. He smiled as he noticed a small note and turned it over.

It was incomprehensible. He didn't know if it was written in the Goblin's native language, or if her spelling and handwriting was just so terrible as to be indecipherable, but decided in the end it didn't really matter. He carefully lifted the tray and pulled out a blank grimoire. A bonus of being a Scribe was the loss of his spellbook would not stop him. He could easily replace it, given time, blank pages, and plenty of the special ink.

He knew his most important task was to study the staff but figured replacing his grimoire should take priority; he was useless without it. So he ate while using a large brush to apply the ink to each page, soaking the pages in swirls of colors, chanting between bites of fruit, and tracing arcane sigils as he went. The end result made each page appear as though it was merely a solid block of stained velum. In truth, he had traced his will and important arcane formulae into each page, crafting a held spell within the grimoire that could be pulled in a moment's notice and used in any way he needed to.

He closed the book and smiled in satisfaction. Ten had done a fantastic job with the creation of the ink, and he would need to thank her in person. But for now, he would turn his attention to the job at hand.

The staff.

STAVES AND RODS

H E LIFTED THE staff and set it on the trunk. It seemed simple enough. Decorative, certainly, but that was not too unusual. Carved from ash and inlaid with veins of opal and gold filigree, the top was rounded and looked as though something could be set within a recess at the very top. It slimmed a little towards the bottom but suddenly broke off. As it was, it was really more of a stave than a staff.

Many nonpractitioners assumed that magic staffs were rare and powerful objects created through painstaking artifice and mad magics. That was rarely the case. Most magic staffs were made when a wizard picked up some fallen limb that looked sturdy enough and began channeling magic through it. Even fancy staffs like this one, with opal inlay and gold filigree, were nothing more than common walking sticks until someone channeled something through them.

But sometimes, very rarely, someone terrifyingly powerful decided to use an object to channel their power and it was changed forever. Charged with arcane might, it became more than a tool; it became capable of magnifying and twisting a mage's abilities to nightmarish levels. Nearly every legendary wizard throughout time had either created such relics in their passing or used them to seal themselves into myth.

He wasn't the greatest history student in the Academy, but any wizard who had created or used such a relic should be in his history books. Dhali lifted the staff and opened his trunk to rummage at the bottom amongst the many books he had brought with him. His sister had called it a waste of space, but now he was relieved he had brought them. He pulled two books out and re-shut the trunk. Opening the first, he began scanning through, looking for St. Viscu or any clue to the staff's history and legend.

Hours later, the tent flap opened and closed, a soft light filling the space. Without turning from his work, Dhali sighed a little, knowing it was pointless to argue. "Hello, Neela."

"Dhalius," she returned, but there was something in her voice, something other than the cold indifference he was used to.

He turned to look at her. She stood there wringing her hands gently at her waist. Even in the dim light, he could see her eyes were watering.

"Neela, what's . . . " he began.

"Thank you for getting her back, for saving Tzacha. I know you—you had to, you had to free yourself and she was there, but if you *hadn't* saved her, or if you had sided with them—" She paused. "But you didn't. She is a friend, so thank you."

"Of course, I only did what any—"

"No. You didn't. Do not pretend that men are somehow . . . that other men are good."

"There are other good men," he argued, but not very strongly.

"Maybe, but they are few, and you are here," Neela said. "We lost too many, my friends and sisters, in this action." She laughed. "I am not good with these things."

He rose and, silently setting the book aside, embraced her. She stiffened for a second, as if surprised by the act, and then relaxed in his arms, returning the embrace. They stayed that way for a few moments before she looked up at him.

"She was captured because of me," he said. "She saved

me, and I returned the favor. I am not perfect, but I am a member of this company, and I couldn't let them have one of ours."

"I came in while you were sleeping. I tended your wounds as best I could," she said, burying her face in his chest. "I wanted to wake you, but you seemed so . . . you needed your sleep." That explained why he had woken so refreshed; it was a kindness he had not known.

"Thank you. I appreciate your touch, Neela," he said.

"I would like to be close."

"To feed?" he asked.

"No, to . . . to be close," she repeated. "Unless you object to me."

"Oh, no, of course not. I just—I'm surprised is all. Of course I'll, uh, be close with you." He smiled.

She sighed in relief and stepped back, reached down to untie her skirt. As it fell to the floor, he was greeted by the sight of a half-rigid phallus. It was not as thick or long as his own, but it would likely make a few men Dhali knew jealous. His jaw fell as he realized what she meant by being close.

"I . . . did not . . . " he started.

"What?"

"You have a cock." He stated the *very* obvious.

"All plants are hermaphroditic," she said, looking at him askance. "Are you changing your mind?" Her voice cracked a bit, as though on the verge of tears.

He looked back at her face. He had never been attracted to men before—well, none that he would have admitted to—but he was surprised to find he was not repulsed, not by her body, nor by the idea. "I, no, I just haven't been . . . I don't . . . "

"I will be gentle if you let me," she promised, and reached forward, her hand trailing the slowly rising shape of his own penis through his robes.

Without responding, he reached down and gently took hold of her, marveling at the warmth he felt in her, the gentle throb as it reacted to his touch. He pulled the skin back, revealing her glans, and gently stroked her, taking a firm grip and moving his hand in slow motions, drawing a small whimper from Neela's throat.

She smiled and reached for him, pulling at his robe. "You're wearing too much," she complained.

He chuckled and stepped back to pull off his clothes. She lifted her blouse above her head at the same time, so when they came back together, they were both fully nude. She reached forward and rubbed her length along his, doing her best to wrap her small hand around both of them to stroke them together.

"Lay on the cot," she commanded.

He nodded, too nervous to speak, aware that this could hurt terribly, but did as she asked. She knelt between his legs, which surprised him, but when her head dipped below his balls and he felt her tongue slide against his ass, he had to bite back a yelp. He reached down to support his legs, unsure what to do with himself. She reached up, her hand reaching around his cock, and she began stroking him gently as she probed with her tongue, licking and exploring him.

The pleasure was nearly blinding as she pushed forward and began swirling her tongue inside him. He tried not to buck, but he found himself biting his lips to stifle his moans. As quickly as it began, it was over and she rose. She angled her cock and pressed it to his ass.

"Breathe, relax, it will . . . sting at first. I will be gentle," she promised again.

He nodded, fear once again flooding his system, and took a deep breath. As he did, she pressed forward, using her hand to guide her pulsing warmth into his ass. His eyes widened as she stretched him out, a little whimper escaping his lips as the pain shot through him.

"Shh, breathe," she cooed. "You are okay?" It was a question and a statement.

After a moment, he nodded. He found his body had

grown used to her. The warmth, the feeling of her inside him, it was not at all unpleasant as he had assumed it would be, other than the painfulness of the stretch.

She nodded and began rocking her hips, gently pushing up and into him. As her pelvis bounced against his butt, a wave of orgasmic pleasure speared through his body, and he found himself gasping for breath. He reached down and wrapped his own hand around his throbbing penis and began to stroke himself, matching the rhythm of Neela's hips.

"Are you okay?" she asked again, a worried look passing over her features as she stopped moving.

"Gods yes. Keep . . . keep going," he nearly begged.

She looked relieved and started her thrusts again, a little harder, a little deeper. Each time she pushed all the way into him, her cock delivered an electric blast of pleasure that he felt from his toes to the top of his skull.

Neela's eyes shut tight as she bucked against him and let out a strangled moan. He felt her shudder and could feel something warm and velvety filling him. He knew he couldn't hold on any longer either. He reached down, grabbing her hand and squeezing it as her thrust took him over the edge and he came hard. His cum splattered across his stomach and chest as he came. Neela pulled out slowly, dragging another groan from him, and began lapping up his spilled seed greedily.

When she was done, she crawled up the cot and lay across him. "I hope it did not hurt too bad," she whispered.

"No, it was wonderful to be close to you," he answered.

"Good, next time, you can do that to me," she said and slowly pulled herself off him. She seemed a little unsteady. It seemed even with this closeness, she would finish their tryst and leave into the night. He wondered if anyone in this company shared more than just physical closeness.

"You could stay with me tonight," he offered.

Neela looked startled at the suggestion.

"I . . . " She shook her head, and he could have sworn

she was blushing in the low light. "No, I have other duties to perform. But maybe some night." She looked down thoughtfully and then turned and left.

He watched her go and slowly rose, wincing as his body protested, but protest or not, he would be damned if he didn't clean himself up before he fell to sleep.

The next morning, Dhalius gingerly sat at one of the tables in the common area, careful to sit on his thighs instead his ass, and set his plate of porridge and fruit down. He was sore, sorer now than he had been last night. He rested his head on his hand and propped himself up on his elbow as he spooned the porridge into his mouth, now used enough to the bland flavor to not make any faces as he ate the stuff. A shadow fell across his plate, and he felt rather than saw someone sit across from him.

"Human." The voice was lilting and musical but somehow still managed to convey a disdain usually reserved for stepping in a dung heap.

He glanced up and saw the Elven ranger that had found them in the forest.

"Palaas," he replied, just barely remembering her name as the person who had stopped him from entering the medical tent.

"I heard you gave yourself to Neela last night." She said it so matter-of-factly, the way one might state that it was cloudy or that water was wet.

Dhalius could feel his cheeks and ears burning as the blush overtook him. He wanted to crawl into his robes and die, but on the other hand, he was exhausted, he had nearly died, and Neela had needed him. His shame was residual. He had no cause for it.

"That hardly seems like your business," he finally said when he had his composure. He looked up to meet her eyes.

"So many of us come here to escape your kind. Men, I mean."

"I figured," Dhali said.

"They've been . . . hurt. Men are the worst thing in this world, and while human men are undoubtedly the worst of them, almost universally, the males of the species are the same. They take, they ravage, they act as though the whole world owes them all they want and that they need give nothing back." Her nails, long and slender, clicked on the wood. "And so it would have seemed with you, enjoying yourself with any number of the members of the outfit, without a care for—"

"I have done nothing that was not—" Dhali objected.

Palaas held up a hand. "No, but you have enjoyed yourself in this place—as a man—that is meant for women."

Dhalius pressed his lips together. He couldn't argue with that, and truth be told, he had been worried that his dalliances would lead to catastrophe. All it would take is one misunderstanding, one miscommunication, and it could lead to his exile or, worse, execution. He wondered if that time had come.

"But giving yourself, not for your pleasure but hers, not for you but fully for the sake of Neela . . . Tell me. Do you consider yourself less of a man now? Do you feel as though being taken by her made you a woman?"

Dhalius bristled at the suggestion. "You insult me, all women, and especially, you insult Neela," he said. "In this place, of all places, what does me being a man matter? I wasn't superior or better than anyone else in this camp before last night, nor would it matter to anyone here if I was a eunuch or some sexless being. Me being a man is irrelevant to my abilities and worth. I have been close to some of my comrades, we have shared a bed for comfort, or for pleasure, or maybe just because they were bored and curious, but it has no impact on anyone's worth. As for Neela, I shared a moment of intimacy with a friend, one we *both* enjoyed. I would do so again if she wishes, and it will not change who I am, nor what I can do for this company."

Throughout his softly spoken tirade, Palaas watched him passively, unimpressed. Finally, when it was clear he was spent, she spoke. "Good. I want to make sure you understand your place, Human. You are a battle mage of the Defiant Host now. Whom you bed or who beds you has no consequence so long as you do your part honestly and with integrity. Your response is heartening. While you are disgusting, and obviously flawed deeply by dint of your very being . . . you are at least a credit to both humans and men." She reached forward and sprinkled *something* over his porridge, and without another word, stood and left, leaving Dhalius staring down at his now tainted breakfast.

"Woooaah!" Ten-Tulips said as she jogged over and jumped up onto the seat next to him, causing the bench to bounce and a small wave of pain to wash through Dhali. "Palaas must *really* like you!"

"What?" Dhali said, looking at his diminutive friend. "She just put . . . stuff on my food!"

"*Elven stuff!*" she exclaimed. "Taste it!"

"It's probably poison," he argued.

"Taaaste it!" she nearly shouted.

Dhali, aware others were beginning to stare, grumbled and brought a small bite of the porridge to his mouth. His eyes widened. "Holy shit, this is delicious!" He shoveled in a few more bites. "What did she do?"

"Elves, man. They got that tasty stuff. I bet it fills you up and makes you feel like you're full and refreshed. I hear they sprinkle it on each other when they—"

"Ten," Dhalius said. "I'm eating."

"I'm talking about when they're eating!" she argued but grinned and fell silent for a second. "Can I try?"

"Yeah, of course." He scooted his plate over, though he was sad to have less of the now decadently delicious gruel to eat for himself.

After breakfast and a brief conversation, Dhalius excused himself and returned to his studies.

ANSWER IN THE DARKNESS

D HALIUS SPENT THE next several days stooped over his trunk, books spread out around him. Each time he felt like he was getting close to an answer, the text would refer him to another book, which in turn would either refer him back to the original text, another book, or, worse, some text he had never heard of or had no way of accessing. When that happened, he had no choice but to follow the threads as well as he could to find the next bit of direction. Nearby, he kept a once blank parchment on which he would jot down notes and a quill.

Surprisingly, his days were *also* filled with visitors. Korska and her squad would come in ones or twos. Always teasing him about how what few muscles he had were wasting away while he wasted time, or sometimes trying to outright convince him to come and train or exercise with them. He was tempted—he was feeling a bit stir-crazy—but he knew Lakista was counting on him. He had taken an immense liking to Henrietta especially. The Dwarf had no manners or tact but was always quick with a joke and would sneak him spiced mead that made his head swim pleasantly after just a few sips.

The women he had helped rescue would occasionally stop by as well, though that seemed more out of obligation than a desire to enjoy his company. But still, he appreciated it, and he did his best to be polite and answer questions. They also brought him food from the mess and fresh water. He had to wonder if it were at Lakista's orders—bring him his food and water under the guise of a visit so he would stay put, out of the way, and hard at work figuring out the puzzle before him. But of course, his most frequent visitor was Ten-Tulips. The Goblin seemed to stop by whenever she wasn't engaged in something else. At first, he found her disruptive, but soon, he realized that if he continued his studies and work, she would lapse into silence and do her own thing. He appreciated that; it allowed him to feel less lonely stuck over his books.

The one person who hadn't come to visit was Neela. He wondered if he had made her uncomfortable or done something wrong by offering his cot to her for the night. Or perhaps now that she had . . . been close to him, she'd had her fill. He reminded himself that she, an Alarune, had a different morality and outlook than him. Still, he had enjoyed her visits and hoped she would come again.

Ten-Tulips was deep in some project in the corner of his tent when he stumbled on the passage he had been searching for for days. "Son of a whore!" he whispered, his finger tracing the words in front of him. He reached for his quill and began writing frantically, glancing between the parchment and the book to make sure he didn't make a mess, nor make any mistakes in his transcription.

"What?" Ten asked.

"Hold on," he commanded.

"What is it?" she asked again, ignoring him.

"Hold *on*" he said again as he read and then reread the passage. He finally looked up. "I need to speak to the captain." He rose and frowned at the parchment, willing the ink to dry faster. "Oh fuck it, I'll take the book."

"Would you tell me what it is?" Ten growled. She had clambered up onto the trunk so she could look him in the eyes. He noticed that her eyes, as large as they were, seemed to almost glow in the shadows cast by his candle.

"We have to do anything we can to keep the staff away from this Goana," he said. "It's a key." He grabbed the book and headed out into the camp. The sudden bright light was almost blinding, and he belatedly realized he hadn't stepped foot outside his tent in days. He squinted at the light and frowned as he realized people were packing the camp up.

"Excuse me, what is happening?" he asked a passing soldier.

"Have you missed the briefing?" she said, looking him up and down with a clear look of disapproval. "The Rotten Eaves are marching. We're to reposition between them and Zachman's crossing before they reach it."

"Oh . . . gods." Dhali turned and started running, book in hand, a finger jammed in the proper page as he made a beeline for where the command tent had been. He realized before he arrived that it was likely Lakista would be packed and overseeing some other area now.

He spotted the Lieutenant Jaxsi towering above a group of women, supervising their work. She had come and crouched inside his tent while she visited, hardly holding any sort of conversation before leaving again. She had seemed intimidated by the sheer number of books he had, and he got the impression that she had come from a community that considered reading, possibly even the ability to read, as something to look on with suspicion.

But he knew her, so he called to her. "Lieutenant Jaxsi!" He waved and hurried over to her.

She looked surprised to see him outside his tent, as though he was somewhere he shouldn't be. She looked around, her wild mane of red curls bouncing as she did.

"Lieutenant Jaxsi," he said again as he reached her. "I'm looking for the captain. Do you know where I can find her?"

Jaxsi had leaned down to hear him better and then rose back over the throng of activity, scanning the camp. Dhalius wasn't the tallest man in the world, and Jaxsi towered over anyone else he had seen in the camp, other than perhaps Korska. After a moment, she leaned back down, making him feel a bit like a child asking for a piece of candy. "She's over there, helping organize our wagons . . . Shouldn't you be packing your tent?"

"Yes," he yelled over his shoulder, already dashing through the camp in the direction Jaxsi had pointed. He should be packing his tent, he realized, but this was too important. He assumed Lakista would forgive him. He *hoped* she was still in a kind mood. He saw her finally, directing the packing of wagons for gear and weapons.

"Captain!" he called.

"Mage," she responded when he finally reached her. "Are you packed? I'm very busy."

"No. No, Captain." He panted and held the book out to her, his finger still jammed between the pages.

She looked at the book and then at him.

"You discovered something?" she asked, taking the book from him and flipping it open.

He was relieved; it seemed that while she hadn't warmed to him at all, she was at least not treating him as a poisonous slug any longer.

"Yes, Captain. The staff would pop up now and then in my books, always in reference to something else. It was always a fragment of the puzzle, something rescued from some tyrant or mad wizard. But mostly, Captain, it is a key, part of a set. I was trying to figure out why St. Viscu was not familiar to me, why he wasn't in any of my texts. But if you trace it all back, you can find that St. Viscu wasn't a mage at all. He was a cleric, a simple healer. He served in a mercenary company during the—"

"I don't need a history lesson, mage," Lakista said, her eyes darkening. "I would appreciate expediency in your blabbering."

He sighed. "During the War of the Last Word," he finished.

Lakista stiffened. There wasn't a mortal alive who didn't know about the War of the Last Word, when the sorcerer king Ektam ascended to godhood and began his campaign to subjugate the kingdoms under his rule. He had opened portals to the Abyss, summoning eldritch horrors and unleashing them upon the mortal races. It was only through a desperate sacrifice of soldiers, mages, and the temple of the god of life, Fele'na, that they were able to stop him, sending him through his own portal and trapping the new godling in the Abyss.

"Viscu was a priest of Fele'na, and according to legend and Felenian lore, his staff, which he channeled the power of the pantheon with to seal the Abyssal portals, then shattered into three parts. Three keys," he finished. The last bit he only discovered in an old prayer book—luckily, his father had been an observant Felenian and made sure all of his children had their own copies of the small tome.

"You think Goana is attempting to free Ektam?" she asked. "She can't be that insane."

"You said it yourself she made a sacrifice in the name of her god. What if Ektam *is* her god? It is possible she wants the staff for its powers, but if she is gathering all three parts, then I think it would be safe to say that she is aiming for godhood herself."

"What? That's a leap, isn't it?" She handed the book back to him. "Going from she serves Ektam to she wants to become a—"

"Captain." He cut her off. "Every evil wizard, every last one, has angled for godhood eventually. It may not start that way, but that greed, that lust for power, it can never be sated, and if she's not already aiming for it, she will. We have to keep the staff away from her at all costs. We should not be marching it directly towards her."

"You want us to retreat?" she scoffed, crossing her arms over her chest.

"I want us to keep the staff away from the ego-maniacal mage who is seeking it," he answered.

She frowned at him and shook her head. "No. We will not flee, leaving Zachman's Crossing defenseless. We will not turn tail and be known as cowards. And we will not let Goana roam free, uncontested."

"Then let's send the staff to a temple of Fele'na, send it away so that it is far from the battle and her hands," he pleaded.

"Can you use it?" she asked suddenly.

"Use it?" he repeated. "You want me to attempt to use it in battle? Bring it right to her?" He stared at her, dumbfounded by what he felt was the lack of foresight.

She glared back, no mercy or leeway in her stare. He could abandon his post, take the staff himself to the temple, but without him, they would be trapped in a magic battle with no mage of their own. It may not consign them all to death, but how many would die? What would become of Korska or Henri on the battlefield? Not to mention Ten and Neela. He swallowed.

"In theory. I can channel magic through the staff, but without ample time to study and master it and understand how it interacts with my spells, I can't do much. I'm a Scribe, Captain, my spellwork relies on ink. The staff may allow me to venture into other schools of magic more easily, but it will not make my combat more efficient, at least . . . not until I have time to practice with it."

"Then I suggest you begin practicing with it while we march to reposition our camp, " she said and turned away from him. "Dismissed."

He stood there for a long moment, frustrated that the enormity of consequences wasn't getting through to the captain. But when it was clear she would not turn around or reconsider, he worked his way back to his tent to begin packing and getting ready for the next march. Mostly, he had to make sure his trunk was on a wagon and that the staff of Viscu was safe.

A MOMENT OF PEACE

T HE MARCH WAS uneventful, giving Dhalius plenty of opportunity to attempt to figure out how to channel his magic through a stave. Channeling was not new to him; his entire discipline was about channeling will and power through ink. But with that, he was manipulating the ink. It was the conduit, the target, and the end result. When working through a stave, he was a bit at a loss.

As he walked, he held one of the vials of ink in one hand and the stave in the other. Ten watched him intently as he pointed the stave at the liquid and chanted. The ink bubbled in its glass tube, his eyes glowed with power, and then . . . nothing.

"Having problems?" Ten asked. She had walked beside him, peering up to watch him as he experimented.

"A little," he admitted. "When I concentrate, my spells go immediately to the ink, bypassing the stave altogether. I'm so conditioned to work with it . . . It's a pretty common issue for Academy mages," he said, frowning. Of course, the Academy would be loath to admit it, but training to such a high level in one school often made mages less capable of being flexible in their spellwork. It was one of the many ways non-Academy mages and wild-witches were superior to the Academy. They may never be as potent, but they were more than capable of becoming adept a wide variety of magics.

"How do you fix that?" she asked. She understood

magic basics, though it was only tangential knowledge for her.

"I don't know. I have to bridge the gap between myself and the stave itself. But because it's old and powerful, it has a sort of will of its own, a personality. It's like taking a new lover," he said offhandedly. "You have to discover what it likes, what it dislikes, how to work in tandem so you can achieve unity."

"Sounds sexy," Ten said.

"It isn't; it's an analogy." He laughed. "But to continue the analogy, Captain Lakista basically created an arranged marriage and told us to conceive on the day we met." He sighed, looking at the stave and rolling his shoulders. "Somehow, I need to mesh it together, make it work." He halfheartedly wiggled the stave a little as though it were a magic wand.

"Too bad it isn't a brush," she said. "Like the one you use to paint those spells in your book."

"A brush," he repeated. "You . . . you might be a genius, Ten!"

"You're just now noticing?" she asked with a wicked grin.

"No, I knew that already, sorry." He laughed. "I need, well, I need hair . . . Horse hair would probably be best for this size," he said, staring at the stave in his hand now.

"Wait, you're serious? You're going to try to turn the evil relic into a paintbrush?" Ten asked.

"It isn't evil. It's just . . . it can be used for evil. Anything can be used for evil, and not a paintbrush, an ink brush. Think about it, Ten. I create that connection between its use, my magic, and its appearance, it should work, but also, if we change the way it looks, maybe we can hide it in plain sight!" He looked around, unsure where the best place to get horse hair would be. "Do you know our stable master?"

"Bolokt an Asher? She'll be further back with all the wagons. Wait, you're going to ask for *her* hair?" Ten asked incredulously.

"What? No—no, Ten, I'm going to ask for horse hair." He shook his head as he laughed and turned to jog down the marching line of the Host to head for the wagons. Ten was brilliant and scattered in equal measures. He would never have thought to turn the staff section into a brush without her. After a few minutes, he spotted the wagons and grinned as he approached them.

"Pardon . . . " he said as he came side by side with a small fae woman riding a horse. Her wings flittered in irritation as she looked down at him, like she had swallowed a bug.

"Why is mage-man?" she asked, her accent strange and ethereal, her cute pert nose wrinkling slightly.

"Why am . . . why am I here?"

"Why is man?" she pushed.

"Well, I suppose I was born that way," he stammered, feeling suddenly lost.

"Was mistake?" she questioned him and then fell silent, watching him with blank curiosity.

"Well, maybe that is true, but . . . Listen, are you the stablemaster?" he asked.

"You want horse?" she returned—he wondered if she could speak without it being in the form of a question.

"Oh, no, I was hoping to acquire some horse hair," he explained. The faerie woman's eyes widened, and she fell forward to grab great armfuls of her steed's mane. "No is for you!" she hissed.

Dhalius raised his hands in defense of her venom. "No, I'm not trying to take *your* horse or your horse's hair. I just . . . are you the stablemaster?"

"No she is not." The voice was deep and sonorous, like a bellow at speaking volume.

When he turned to face the voice, he suddenly understood Ten's confusion. A Centaur cantered up to them and then fell into a trot beside them both. She was a striking figure, standing at least eight feet tall from hoof to head. Her body was well muscled, with skin the color of caramel and black cascading hair. She wore a top of leather straps and matching arm braces but required no other clothing for her modesty. "She is one of the attendants. What do you want, human?"

"The man-mage wants hair!" the fae cried again.

"You don't look bald," the Centaur said, raising a fine eyebrow over her deep, dark eyes.

"I, well, no, you must be Bolokt, honored to meet you." He wasn't sure if he should offer her his hand or bow, so he settled on just giving a deep nod. "My name is—"

"Dhalius, I know. You've made quite the impression." She paused. "Here, get on." She offered her hand.

He had never ridden a Centaur before and felt a bit nervous, but he didn't want to appear like a bumpkin due to his inexperience so took her hand and let her haul him onto her back. Unsure what to do with himself, he placed his hands near the juncture where human met horse and steadied himself.

"You are having problems fitting in still?" Bolokt asked, trotting a bit away from the line as to give them some privacy.

"Some. I am still something of a pariah, if I am to be honest, but I am slowly making friends," he admitted.

"Yes, and your actions have warmed many to your presence. I heard about the rescue after our battle. Very impressive." Bolokt glanced over her shoulder at him. "And while many in the Host despise men, there are those that are not opposed to a handsome one amongst us, if for nothing else than to enjoy the sight. Maybe wear less or tighter clothes," she suggested.

"Uh. Thank you." He coughed. "I was looking for you because I was hoping that I could procure some hair from one of the horses' manes. It would assist in my magic and hopefully serve the Host."

Bolokt reached up and pulled her hair up, tying it in a quick ponytail, giving him a perfect view of her strong and attractive back. "While I am aware my locks are very attractive, I am going to assume you're not asking to shave me."

"No, I meant from one of the horses, not from you." He chuckled.

"Hmm, I don't see the harm," she said after a long pause. "Though I prefer to partake of an exchange of services. Ah, that's it. You haven't been assigned a duty detail yet, have you?"

"I . . . " Dhalius paused. "I suppose I haven't. I've been so busy fighting and researching that I haven't actually fallen into the flow of life in the camp."

"Then we can assign you to the stable work detail. Do you have any experience?"

He chuckled, wondering if she was planning on giving him one of the less desirable jobs like scooping manure. "Plenty, I grew up on a farm, and my uncle was a farrier for the local town. I assisted him. I would not call myself adept, but . . . I'm no stranger."

"A farrier?" Bolokt stopped and turned to face him as fully as she was able—he was surprised at how flexible her spine was. "That is serendipitous, as we lost our last one. I'll speak to Lakista and Joachima, our blacksmith. Get you trained and then assigned."

"That sounds good. It would be good to help the company more and, honestly, get out of my tent and away from my books for a minute. Labor would help keep me in fighting shape."

"Good, I look forward to working with you, Dhalius. Tell me, how did a farmhand grow to become a mage?"

Dhalius spent the rest of the march on the back of Bolokt discussing each other's past and experiences. He had very little chance to encounter Centaur before, and it was an interesting time learning about her nomadic culture and experience. When they had made it through to the other side of Zachman's passing, they parted ways, with Bolokt reminding him she would speak to the captain about his assignment. Dhalius was fine with that. He watched the women unpacking and setting up, looking for any friendly faces. Eventually, he saw Ten and decided she would be as close to a friendly neighbor as he could ask for, since he could not find his squad. He set his pack down and pulled out his tent to begin setting up.

A few hours later, Dhalius was amazed at the speed and efficiency of the Host. To break down, march, and redeploy so quickly was a feat he would not expect from an organized military, let alone a mercenary company. He had just pushed his trunk back into the tent and finished setting up the cot when he felt the heavy hand of Korska fall on his shoulder.

"Come, we're going to the river."

He glanced up at her, a warm blush creeping across his ears as he remembered their last time at the river, then he noticed the rest of her squad.

"We?" he asked.

"We," she agreed and began walking, gently pushing him with her.

"I'm not sure the rest of your squad wants to see or be seen in that state—" he began.

"We're all adults, Dhalius," she said with a chuckle. "We spoke about it after you came back from the ruins. It was ridiculous that they did not treat you in the medical tent."

While he appreciated her words, he still felt that thrill of uncertain nervousness, not to mention a bit of disappointment—he would certainly prefer more one-on-one time with the green amazon. But this would be a good practice. As she said, they were all adults. He could be around them without letting his eyes stray, without showing arousal; he could. He would prove it.

When they arrived at the river, Dhalius quickly stripped and dove into the water, ignoring the hoots and hollers about his ass from the others. The water was bracingly cold, refreshing after the long day. He pointedly avoided looking at the shore as the women followed suit, instead trying to guess by the sound of them diving in who was who. The giant splash was Henrietta, the soft slide was likely Tawna, the water sizzled slightly as Gisla stepped into the shallows, and the heavy splashes were Korska stepping into the water.

His cock stirred slightly at the thought of her, imagining the way the water would shine on her dark green skin, and the contrast between the hard muscles and soft curves threatening to make him stand at attention.

He saw her shadow, identifiable by the mohawk, a moment before her heavy breasts pushed against his back. "What are you doing all the way over here, Dhali? Don't want to spent time with us?"

"Just want to make sure you all have your privacy," he said, looking over his shoulder at her. She was leaning down, pressing against him so as he turned his cheek, it was pressed against hers.

"Dhali." Her hand reached around him, rubbing down his chest and stomach to take hold of his cock. "If I wanted privacy, I would not have invited you."

"But . . . I don't think the others want to . . . watch us." He breathed as slowly as he could as she began to stroke him under the water. "Gods I want to, been thinking about you since—"

"Since I washed you? Been thinking about this too." She squeezed him. "Hey!" She suddenly turned and raised her voice. "Any of you care if I fuck our mage here?"

"Korska!" Dhalius hissed, but it was too late. The others called a number of nonplussed answers.

"Now, if *you* aren't interested, that's fine. But your body is telling me you are."

He breathed deeply to take control of himself, as well as calm his nerves, and turned to face her.

She grinned down at him. "I love how hung you are, Dhali. Now, take your big dick, and fuck me."

He grinned wickedly. "Is that an order, Sergeant?" he asked, reaching under the water to massage the folds of her pussy, his fingers deftly parting her labia to massage her clit. At the same time, he leaned forward and sucked her left nipple into his mouth, toying with her nipple ring with his tongue.

She bucked a little and chuckled throatily as she continued to stroke him. "You know I'm a big girl. Your fingers are not going to cut it for me right now." She dragged him by his cock over to some river rocks and turned her back to him, lowering herself to her hands and knees. "Now, do you need me to repeat that order?"

Dhalius considered defying her. He wanted nothing more than to bury his face in her pussy and lap at her juices. "You have the most perfect ass, Korska." He stepped up behind her, brought his hand down hard, slapping her ass, watching it bounce and turn red. She moaned a little. Encouraged, he used his left hand to massaged her, his finger gently rubbing her clit in a small circle as his right hand squeezed her ass. "You're damned beautiful," he said, forgetting the audience they had entirely.

"Stop teasing. In me. Now."

He nodded and guided himself to her pussy and pushed, marveling at how slick she was. No oils, no saliva, he easily slipped into her. Immediately, her muscles squeezed as though she were massaging his cock using nothing but her vaginal muscles. He pushed slowly forward until the entire length of his dick disappeared, swallowed by her body. For a moment, he reveled in the view, her taut muscular back, the vision of her breasts from the side, the contrast of their skin tones against one another. She pushed back against him as if trying to get even more. He encouraged her by pulling back and ramming back in, each thrust taking him from nearly falling out of her to slamming against her. With every move, her ass jiggled against his stomach and his balls slapped against her. He grabbed ahold of her hips to steady himself, and he fucked her, spurred on by her moans and shouts.

"Fuck, yes. Yes, there, keep going!" she commanded.

He let go with his right hand, reaching around her to wrap his fingers around her throat, squeezing gently as he rocketed into her again and again.

"Fuck, I'm cumming!" she cried out, spasming against him. Her pussy squeezed him, twitching around his cock, and she pushed her hips so hard against him that he lost his footing and fell back. "Oh!" she exclaimed, looking back in surprise. Dhali sat in the water panting, his rigid cock, slick with her juices, jutting above the water. "Fuck!" she repeated, frustrated, but then smiled. "Now, my turn to get you off." She grinned and stood, reaching down to lift him out of the water.

"Korska!" he shouted as she manhandled him, but there was little he could do. She put him down on one of the river rocks and knelt between his knees.

"You seem to like my breasts, don't you Dhali?" she asked him.

"Very much. Yes," he agreed, his excitement growing as she lifted her breasts and used them to encompass his erection.

"Good, enjoy them," she said as she placed her hands on either side of her tits and squeezed them together.

She began bouncing them with her hands. Dhali leaned back, using his hands to steady himself as he entered heaven. He couldn't believe how soft and pillowing the feeling of her breasts swallowing his cock was. He looked up just in time to see Korska dip her head and swallow the top of his cock as she continued to massage him with her breasts. The way her soft lips dragged across his skin and how her tusks perfectly framed his dick was almost too much.

He clenched his ass, trying to hold on; it was too good to end so soon. He was so focused on Korska that he didn't notice the others had come closer until Gisla's warm hand touched his thigh.

"I would like a taste," she said, to Dhali's utter surprise and delight.

Korska pulled her head back, letting Dhali's penis free with a pop, but she did not stop bouncing her breasts around him, instead just angling him so Gisla could share. Gisla leaned down, swallowing the tip and running her tongue under the ridge of his glans, her red hair cascading down his thigh as she bobbed her head.

Another hand stroked his chest. Surprised, he turned and saw Henrietta watching intently, hearing him panting. She pulled his head towards her and pushed her tongue into his mouth in a deep kiss. Her lips were soft and full and pressed against his hungrily. She tasted slightly of honeyed mead and made his head spin as they kissed. He moaned as the three women had their way with him,

He felt the pressure building and knew he could last no longer. He pulled back from Henri's passionate kiss. "I'm going to cum," he croaked. Gisla pulled away and ducked out of sight, but a second later, he felt her hot tongue run across his balls.

Korska held his held his gaze, not breaking eye contact. "Do it. Give me your cum," she demanded. "I want it."

The sight and her words pushed him over the edge, and he convulsed, his balls tightening. He geysered cum over Korska's breasts and across her face, splurting stream after stream of hot jizz onto her. He collapsed back into Henrietta, feeling like he might pass out. When he looked up, Korska and Gisla were licking the cum off of Korska's tits.

"No, this is heaven. I definitely died and went to heaven," he panted.

Henrietta laughed as she lowered him to the rock to jump back in the water. "Yer an easy one to please, then."

"Get back in the water, Dhali. Now that we're satiated, we can bathe and focus on other things."

Dhali smiled, his head swimming pleasantly, and rose to do just that when the sound of someone clearing their throat from shore made him jump out of his skin.

Another Dwarven woman, older and more scarred than Henri, stood on the shore, her impressive arms crossed over her chest. "I was told Dhalius had come here to get cleaned up, not to make a mess," she growled.

"Settle!" Henrietta shouted back. "Just some fun."

"Fun's over," the older Dwarf said. "Get dressed, mage, then follow me."

Dhalius swallowed and glanced at the others before hurrying to the shore to hastily get dressed and follow after the grumpy Dwarf, who was already stomping away.

PAINTING THE BATTLEFIELD

"**W**HAT HAPPENS NOW?" Dhalius asked, realizing in the back of his mind that he had asked the same thing to Korska last time they were at the river.

"We're walking back to camp," the Dwarf said curtly.

"No, I mean . . . you're going to tell the captain about . . . about what we were doing," Dhalius explained.

"What? Gods no. Ye think the captain wants to hear about ye having sex? Ye human men have a mighty high expectation of yer own worth!"

"No, I . . . " he stuttered, trying to formulate the question. "I understand there will be consequences, but I hope it will not look bad of Korska or her—"

"Consequences?" The Dward stopped to look at him and then erupted into laughter. "Dhalius, this ain't a convent. We ain't nuns. Sure, lots o' the mercs and women come here to be free o' male domination and leadership, and why not? Boisterous, loud, sure o' their own self-importance, ye lot are exhausting! But no one is expected to be celibate."

"I . . . " He hadn't realized he had been thinking of the Host in exactly those terms until now. "So . . . it's okay?"

"Likely better!" the Dwarf laughed. "Half the Host sneaks off during their off hours, trekking to the nearest town to find a good prick to ride. A year or two back, Lakista had to proclaim that husbands were off limits, afore the angry wives and dads, ye see. Aye, there be a good number o' women in the host that sworn off men, who think yer all trash, and a few number that prefer the company o' other women. I myself am counted in that camp. But no, fuckin' is natural, and no one is going to get on yer case for that. Well, unless ye start sirin' little ones. Not much o' a fightin' force if people are in the motherly way. Hard to swing a sword over a belly. Not impossible, though. Does happen occasionally. Just be careful o' that and ain't no one gonna bat an eye."

Dhalius breathed a sigh of relief. He had been wringing his hands for the last week worrying that his dalliances would have him put to the sword.

"Ain't a single one o' those ladies down there were virginal before ye came, and not a one o' em will swear off the man-meat if ye leave temorrow."

"So . . . wait, why am I in trouble, then?" he asked, furrowing his brow as they resumed walking.

"Trouble? Yer not in any trouble, least not that I know o'it. Not yet at least. But ye been assigned te me, an' I don't like dawdlers. So ye show up on time, ye do yer work, and we're fine."

"You're Joachima!" he nearly shouted.

"Aye."

"The blacksmith."

"Aye," she repeated. "Joachima Vanberg, at yer service." She smiled and patted the hammer that hung by her side. Now that he was no longer sure he was about to be kicked out of the Host or executed, he realized she was *obviously* the blacksmith. Her hands were calloused, and she wore a heavy leather apron covered in soot. She had the fire-reddened skin he had seen on all career smiths before.

"Wait, Vanberg, that's—" he said, realizing she shared a name with—

"Yup, Henrietta is my daughter," she confirmed. "Told ye it were possible to fight while with child."

Dhalius felt himself blushing hard. He had never been

caught in the act before, and to be caught in such a lewd group act by the *mother* of one of the participants was a bit much, even if she seemed to not be fazed.

"I thought you said you preferred the company of women?" he asked "Oh, that's . . . I'm sorry that's probably very personal . . . "

"It is, but it's okay. Yer curious; curiosity is good. Can't do shit with an ignorant person don't want te learn. My marriage were arranged between me and another clan. Birthed Henri, and then when my sack o'shit husband startin' eyein' other women, women he said may produce a male heir, well, that's when I took Henri and headed for the hills. Worked in a few outfits but joined up with the Host near a decade ago, back when the captain's predecessor were in charge."

Dhalius didn't know how to respond to that. He had been thinking of the women of the Defiant Host as a monolith, that those who were kind to him were rare exceptions. Speaking to Joachima now, he realized there was no standard to which the mercenary company came together. While he was the only man in the company, he was just one more individual in a large troop of individual people.

"I look forward to brushing up on my skills with you, Master Joachima," he finally said. "I was telling Bolokt that it would be good to get away from my books and to give more back to the company."

"Good, keep that energy, and I won' care if ye fuckin' *marry* the lot o'em."

As they neared camp, they saw a flourish of activity. Women were throwing on their armor and rushing to get weapons. Joachima grabbed the arm of a nearby soldier. "What is happening?"

"Raiders! Maybe connected to the Eaves!" the woman shouted before pulling away to rush off to arm herself.

"Is there never a peaceful moment in the Host?" Dhalius asked Joachima, only to find she was already rushing off to her own weapons. Dhalius stood for a moment, watching the chaos unfold around him, before realizing he himself was unprepared for what was happening and dashed for his tent.

Getting inside, he nearly tripped over Ten-Tulips, who was sitting on the floor next to his trunk with the staff of Viscu in her hands.

"Ten? What are you doing?" he asked, startled, and even more confused, to see her holding the staff.

"I . . . well, Bolokt was looking for you. She had some . . . " She gave up trying to explain and held the staff up to him.

He stared in near shock. She had been using thin wire to weave the horsehair into something that roughly looked like a brush. It was inexpertly made, but it was a start and would greatly speed his own work.

"You were making the inkbrush!" he exclaimed, taking it from her and examining it. It was very rough. He wouldn't be able to actually use it for calligraphy, and in truth, it looked like something a child would use as their first tool.

"Do you like it?" Ten asked from his hip, grinning up at him.

"Ten, I love it! I could kiss you!" He grinned, then set it back down as he pulled the heavy chain that held his spellbook out of his trunk and looped it around his waist, locking it in place with a heavy padlock. He lifted the newly made brush up and studied it another second. It may not work, or might not work perfectly, but there was no better time to try than now. He grabbed a few flasks of ink, jamming them into his pockets, and looked at Ten. "Ready to defend the camp?"

The two of them began running through the camp, following the throng of warriors towards the imminent battle. There was something electric in the air, something potent. The energy of the combined Host, eager for bloodshed, to earn their reputation as one of the most successful mercenary companies in the kingdoms, was palatable. They were exhausted from the relocation, but they were tired of the lack of action.

By the time they reached the front lines, they were both out of breath. Ten's hood had fallen back, revealing a wild mane of black hair streaked with yellow to match her skin. She bent over and held her knees as she panted. Dhalius smiled and turned his attention to the battle preparations around them.

"Mage," Captain Lakista said, approaching on horseback. "Where is Korska?" she snapped.

"I left her and her squad back at the river, Captain. I'm sure she's been back to camp and is on her way by now." At least he hoped she was.

The captain frowned and scanned the horizon, where the first signs of the encroaching raiders were beginning to appear. "And the staff?"

Dhalius gestured to the newly crafted inkbrush tucked into his chain belt. "I think I can use it. But I cannot promise its effects . . . I am not sure it will be a good idea to use it in the thick of fighting."

"Baptism of fire, then." She turned her steed away.

"Captain, it could be dangerous—" he protested.

"You have your orders, mage. Use the staff. See if we can use her weapons against Goana and her Rotting Eaves. I have no use for cowards." She gave him one last look and rode down the line to continue preparing.

Dhalius looked down at the stave at his waist and then at the oncoming horde. It seemed he had no choice.

The battle raged around Dhalius, bloody and brutal. The raiders rode large wargs, bestial war wolves that were just as dangerous as the mounted warriors on top. Still, the Defiant Host held its own. Dhalius wove his spells, conjuring floating weapons and lashes of barbed ink that flew through the battlefield, tearing riders off their wargs and cutting the limbs off those that charged. Sweat soaked his robes. He found himself near the Elven rangers. They moved in a strange choreography through the battlefield, able to draw arrows and fire in close combat in a mesmerizing way.

As he grew tired, his ability to form fine shapes and weapons flagged. An axe whizzed by his head, and instinctively, he threw out a blast of ink that enveloped his attacker and slammed the man into the ground. A second later, the man's life was ended by an arrow used like a dagger and slammed into his eye socket. Dhalius turned to thank the Elf and saw a spear sailing for her throat. Without thinking, he threw out his hand and formed a shield around her. The spear sank into the ink and stuck. When his shield faded, the Elf looked surprised but nodded her thanks and dove back into the fray. Dhalius was about to follow suit when an earth-shaking roar rattled the battlefield.

In the distance, a massive rotting hound, easily the size of a wagon, charged through the melee, throwing raiders and Defiant mercs into the air. "Gods," Dhalius whispered. The presence of such a terrifying undead beast surely pointed towards their allegiance to the House of Rotting Eaves. He reached down and felt the warmth of the stave at his hip. It was now or never.

"Can you get me closer to that thing?" he shouted at the Elves.

"Closer?" one hissed—he thought it might be Palaas, but he couldn't be sure.

"I have to try to stop it!" he called back.

The Defiant Host didn't have any war beasts to field, and without siege equipment, their only hope was a magical attack. The Elf cursed in her native language and nodded. The unit of Elves moved, keeping Dhalius in the center as they carved a bloody swath through the battlefield toward the beast. Dhali lifted the stave from his belt and concentrated on it. He could swear he could hear it whispering in his skull, words that dripped with spidery arcane energy, begging to be released, begging to be . . . unleashed.

"This is as close as we get, mage," one of the Elves called over the sound of ringing steel.

He nodded; it was enough. He pushed through them and ran full tilt away from the group, right towards the terrifying behemoth. As he ran, he grabbed a vial of ink from his pocket and lifted the stave with his other hand. He opened his mouth, and words he did not know, ancient before the kingdoms were young, poured from his mouth. The stave in his hand quivered, growing so hot he thought it might melt to his skin, a violet light growing and swirling like a tempest around him.

His approach did not go unnoticed. Raiders fell back from the arcane light, but not the beast. It turned its milky, baleful gaze to him, let out a horrid wheezing screech, and bounded towards him. Dhalius did not stop. He reared back and threw the vial with all his might. Clutching the stave with both hands, he pointed it at the beast and screamed the words of a spell he had no way of knowing, praying it would finish before the thing finished its charge.

The beast leapt through the air, bearing down on Dhalius, its foul jaws agape, ready to tear the mage in half. The last word spilled from his lips as the vial smashed into the side of the thing's head. For a moment, all was silent and still. The violet light that had grown around Dhalius constricted into a needle point at the top of the horse hairs.

The beast descended through the air.

And then the inky mess on its face exploded.

It expanded rapidly in a baleful black orb. With each second, it pulsed to grow, everything it touched ripped apart and thrown across the battlefield like so much debris.

Dhalius held on to the staff, trying to control the magic as it ripped through him and fed into the orb. He could feel blood leaking from his nose and ears as it sought to pulverize his mind. He screamed through his teeth, forcing his will on the orb, commanding it to shrink, to dissipate.

He could hear booming laughter from the staff echoing inside his skull. And then . . . and then something brilliant, warm, and *kind* slammed into his psyche, something he could only feel as . . . life.

As quickly as the orb had expanded, it constricted into a ball the size of a fist and flew through the air back towards the staff. Less than a breath later, it slammed into Dhalius's chest, throwing him like a rag doll through the air. Mercifully, he was unconscious before he hit the ground.

RECOVERY

DHALIUS AWOKE SLOWLY. Every part of his body hurt, especially his chest. He groaned and reached up to rub it and immediately regretted the decision. Raising his arms had been agony, but touching his chest? He had no words to describe how it hurt.

"He's awake!" someone nearby shouted. "Call Neela!"

"Call the captain!" someone else shouted.

"Korska requested—" A third voice.

"Korska isn't in charge!" the second voice snapped.

Dhalius cracked open his eyes, or tried to; only the left one responded to his efforts. Looking around from his prone position, he saw several other cots in a large well-lit tent. On all the other cots were women wrapped in bloody bandages, nursing wounds, or, in some cases, covered from head to toe. Casualties of the battle.

"Welcome to the waking world, mage," the captain's voice said from above him. He did his best to turn his head and look up. "Leave us," she commanded, and he could hear the sound of footsteps walking away. "We're alone. Do you have any words for me, mage?"

"Words for you?" he asked, confused. "I . . . What happened? Did we repel them?" He realized it was a stupid question. If they had lost, she would have surely left him on the battlefield to rot.

"We did," she said curtly. "Anything else?"

He swallowed. He wanted to ask for water—he felt like he hadn't had a drink in years, and speaking hurt like razors in his throat. "I am sorry," he finally said. "I couldn't control it. I dropped the . . . I lost the stave, and I can't . . . " He didn't want to think of how many of the company had died as the magic spiraled out of control.

"You're sorry?" She sounded shocked. "First of all, you didn't drop the stave, you were clutching it to your chest when you landed. Hell, the medics had to pry your fingers off it to even treat you."

"Thank Fele'na," he breathed.

"You saved many lives that day, Dhalius. You may have lost control, but you destroyed that monster completely. Without their beast, the rest of the raiders scattered and fell to our archers quickly. If you hadn't, we would have had to retreat; the death toll would have been . . . too great to bear." She sounded like she wanted to say something else but decided against it. "You are proving to be worth your weight in coin, mage," she said instead. "I'll let my sister know you are no longer in danger of dying and are ready for another attempt at healing magic." Captain Lakista turned without another word and began to walk away.

He wanted to stop her, to ask what she meant by her sister, but the words died on his lips, too tired and parched to get them out. Healing magic was wonderful, but it could not solve all problems. For those on the cusp of death, whose injuries were too grievous or whose wounds were caused by magic, it was often ineffectual. Only the greatest miracle workers could overcome these limitations, and almost all of them were high priests working miracles in the biggest temples of the Kingdoms.

He turned his head, scanning the room as best he could with one eye swollen shut. Not only was every cot filled but there were women on the floor and sitting against the walls of the tent. A terrible battle to be sure. Worse still, he could see the remnants of ink on several of the women, victims of his loss of control. He turned his attention to the medics and healers who walked between the rows of cots, searching for Neela, but he could not spot her. With worry and guilt weighing heavy on his heart, he fell back into sleep.

Unsure of how much time had passed, he was woken up by the sound of harsh whispers.

"You told me he was awake." He recognized Korska's voice.

"He did wake up, spoke to the captain, then passed back out." He thought he recognized the other voice as one of the medics.

"Korska," he croaked.

"Hey!" Her voice came closer. "Dhali, how are you feeling?"

He cracked his eyes open, surprised when both worked. He smiled with cracked lips and coughed. "Never better." Korska chuckled. "But could use something to drink."

Korska wore leather leggings and a loose crème-colored blouse that complimented her dark green skin beautifully. When she leaned over him, the collar fell opened, giving him more than an eyeful of her chest.

"I'll get him some water," the medic—an older woman wrapped in bloodied white linens—said, and hurried off.

"You missed the fun," he whispered to her.

"Most of it," Korska admitted. "We arrived just in time to watch you blow yourself up. Even Gisla was impressed with that one."

"That was my goal, impress Gisla," he said and blinked as the medic returned with a bowl for him to drink from. He slowly tried to push himself up. He felt weak and bruised, but gone was the terrible agony he had been in before. He realized a healer must have seen to him while he slept.

"Hey now!" Korska moved forward and supported him, helping him rise to sitting. "Here, let me." She took the bowl from the medic and brought it to Dhali's lips. Again, he was shocked by how gentle she could be. His entire perception of the Orcish race had been that they were cunning brutes, living for battle with little care for elegance or subtlety. Korska was a study in how little he actually knew about the world.

He drank deeply and pulled back. "Gods, that feels good." He looked up at the medic, who stood a few feet away. "When can I return to duties? To my tent?"

"I should ask Neela, but truthfully, tonight if you feel up to it. We are short on beds."

"Don't bother Neela. I am sure she is busy," he said, still feeling anxious that she had not visited since their night together. "Korska can help me to my tent, and you have done more than enough for me already."

"Only *you* are sure you are well enough," the medic pressed, but she looked relieved. He could tell she was either uncomfortable with his presence or just desperate for one less person to watch after. But either way, he was grateful for all they had done and was eager to lighten their load.

"I am positive." He smiled and looked to Korska for help up.

"Do you want me to carry you?" she asked with a smirk.

"I think I'll keep some of my dignity intact, thank you," he responded as she gripped his arm and gently pulled him to his feet. There were several gasps from the room as the sheet covering him fell to the ground, leaving him exposed.

"Don't think that will be a problem." Korska grinned.

"Gods," Dhali whispered, turning red and reaching down to grab the sheet and wrap it around his waist. "Can we just go?"

"We can," she agreed.

He wrapped an arm around her waist, leaning on her heavily. He held the sheet around his hips with his free hand, and the two of them made their way out of the medical tent and through the camp.

The camp was somber. The battle had been too close, too deadly for anyone's liking, and they had still not faced the main force of the Rotting Eaves. As they walked, he noticed he was drawing stares, almost as many as when he had first joined the company. He imagined they were stares of condemnation. He had proven them right, his loss of control on the battlefield proving every hatred they had for men correct.

"Do you want to stop at mess? Get some food?" Korska asked.

"I'm naked, Korska," he reminded her.

"I don't mind." She chuckled.

He sighed and smiled. "Do you ever think of anything other than sex or fighting?"

"Not if I can help it!" she responded quickly.

"You're incorrigible," he reprimanded her with a chuckle.

Getting back to his tent, she helped him sit down on the cot and pushed open his trunk to find something for him to wear. "Don't you have anything other than robes?"

"Bolokt suggested a change in wardrobe . . . " he admitted. "But no, not yet."

"Bolokt is right." She snorted and turned back to him. "Do you need anything else?"

"No I should be—" He choked mid-sentence as she returned to his side, pushed his sheet down, and wrapped her hand around his shaft, slowly stroking it. "Korska—I don't know if I'm up for, well, this."

"You don't need to be. Let me take care of you." She lowered her head, running her tongue across the underside of his cock, tracing the vein from the base to the tip, and looked back up into his eyes.

"Incorrigible." He repeated his remark from earlier as he leaned his head back.

"I have yet to hear a single complaint from you, mage," she accused as she bent back down to administer several kisses up and down his length, then licked him again, her hand never stopping or slowing.

"Why?" he suddenly asked. "If you enjoy sex so much,

why join a mercenary group of women? And why me? You could certainly enjoy any man you came across."

"You want to talk instead?" she asked, not slowing.

"I don't want you to stop," he answered, his eyes locked on to the motion of her hand.

"Hmm," she responded, resuming her kisses. "I wanted to see the world, and I wanted to fight with the best. My people are great warriors, survivors, but they stick to our jungles. I wanted more," she said between licks and kisses. "As for why you . . . first, most men outside of my jungles aren't able to measure up to what I need." She sat up, pulling the laces of her blouse open and tugging the fabric down so her breasts spilled out. "I chose you at first because you were a new comrade in arms, and I was horny; it seemed an easy choice. You are not unattractive to look at, and I prefer the real thing to the prosthetics that some of the women enjoy using." She pressed herself against him lightly, dragging her breasts against his stomach. He felt intoxicated by the way they bounced against him as she continued to stroke his cock with both hands. "I was surprised by what you were packing, to be sure, but more than that, you're a far cry from the clumsy and selfish fucking most trysts involve."

"I just want you to enjoy it as much as I do." He gasped, feeling himself getting close to the point of no return.

"No. You're selfish too. You *enjoy* giving almost as much as getting. That's what sets it apart for you. It isn't a chore, you're excited by it, and that makes it exciting to give it back to you."

He didn't answer, his hips writhing under her. He closed his eyes. He didn't need to warn her, or say anything at all, they both knew he was at the limit. She pulled her hands to the base of his cock and bent down to swallow his head, rolling her tongue over, under, and around the glans. Dhali brought his arm to his mouth to stifle a shout as he came.

She did not stop sucking, greedily swallowing every

drop of cum. He shuddered, the intense sensitivity of post-orgasm almost painful under her administrations. Finally, she pulled back, letting his cock fall out of her mouth, and sat up, wiping her chin and smiling. She pulled her shirt back up and began tying it closed.

"When I feel better, as soon as I am capable, I am going to spend a full day pleasuring you, Korska," he promised. "I'll bury my face in your—"

"There you go being selfish again." She winked. "I'll keep you to that promise, but for now, get some rest. You'll be expected to return to your duties as soon as you're able." Her face fell into a dark seriousness. "And we don't know when the Rotting Eaves will resume their advance. If nothing else, this last battle proved we were overconfident. We'll need you at your best." She smiled again, trying to alleviate the morose note she was leaving on. "I'm sure the rest of the squad will be by to check on you soon. Get some rest."

In the morning, Dhalius rose feeling sore, still not fully healed, but damned if he would languish in bed even another hour. He made his way to the mess, grabbing just a bit of bread and an apple, and made his way to the mobile forge to check in with Joachima, mostly to inform her he would be back as quickly as possible. Pulling the hood of his robes over his head, he headed out of camp without speaking to anyone else, to make his way to Zachman's Crossing. It was his first time entering the city on his own, his first time not marching through with the company. He was surprised to see so many women of the Host in town. They were shopping or running other errands. He saw more than a few throwing furtive glances this way and that, and remembered what Joachima had said about the nocturnal activities of many of the mercenaries.

He smiled; it was none of his business. After some asking around, he found the local seamstress and leatherworkers and set about acquiring clothes more suited to camp life than his Academy robes. He had yet to be paid from the Host's coffers but had brought some coin he had saved up. When he made his way back to camp, he did so with a fresh bundle under his arm and wearing new trousers and a shirt. It felt almost strange to be dressed so mundanely. But it made him feel less like he stuck out like a sore thumb, and the idea of working in a forge in big flowy robes sounded like a fantastic way to set himself on fire. As he neared the gates of the camp, the guards crossed their halberds to bar entrance . . . until they realized who he was.

He chuckled as he walked through camp. He was drawing as many stares now as he had when he first joined the ranks of the Host. Now, it was surprise and outrage followed by quiet acceptance when they recognized him. A few women, people he had spoken to through the last weeks, even complimented him, saying the look suited him. He dropped his new wardrobe off in his tent and then made his way to Joachima to begin his training.

SLICE OF LIFE

DHALIUS FELL INTO a comfortable rhythm in the camp. He would wake and get breakfast, then head to the forge to repair or make horseshoes and nails. After noon, he would head to the stables to help reshoe horses and care for any of their needs. He found the company of both Joachima and Bolokt pleasant, though both were strict masters and brooked no shortcuts or dalliance.

After a day of toiling in the forge and working with the animals, Dhali would head to the river to scrub the sweat and dirt from his body. He was growing stronger through the labor, regaining some of the color and muscle he had lost in his years at the Academy. It mattered less and less whether he was alone or not. If there were women bathing he did not know, he would trek further down the river and wash away the grime in private. He continued enjoying Korska's company frequently on these trips, occasionally joined by Gisla and Henrietta, and on one occasion even Tawna, though he got the impression that for her, it was curiosity more than an actual desire to engage with the mammals.

Once he was clean, *or* once his squad mates were satiated, he would head back to camp and join in drills with the squad, moving through combat maneuvers and sparring with shields and dulled blades until each group was well versed enough in the company and squad tactics to work as a seamless unit. Dhalius knew that in the field, this would be different; in the field, he would have his spellbook open and he would be calling upon the arcane might of the staff to battle other mages. But he also knew the importance of being able to gut an adversary and cover his comrades with shield and sword.

In the evenings, he would eat his dinner while continuing his studies of the stave and other arcane matters. These sessions were usually conducted either in his own or in Ten-Tulips' tent. She would spend the time bent over her alchemical work, muttering formulae with various devices while grinding herbs and mixing strange potions over a small flame.

One night, it was getting late, and Dhalius stretched. "Gods, I never thought I'd say it, but I am tired of waiting for orders."

"Antsy?" Ten asked, glancing up from her work desk.

"A bit. There's only so much that theory and supposition can do. Until I have a chance to test my magic in a real fight . . . " He trailed off.

"You need to stretch your magical legs," she said.

"Exactly!" he exclaimed.

"Well, let me ask: your magic, you can form anything with it?" She watched him, something strange in her expression.

"Yes, usually phantasmic monsters or weapons make the most sense, but I suppose there aren't any real limits other than the amount of—"

"So you could make rope or chains . . . if you wanted?" she pressed.

"Well, yes," he said, confused by her questions.

"Have you ever"—her eyes grew almost as big as her grin, glowing softly in the dim light of the tent—"used them to tie up a woman? You know, hold her in the air while you do it?"

"Ten! No, Gods no, I'm no—I would never force a woman into such a position. I don't force myself on—"

"I'm not saying force yourself. I'm saying it can be fun.

You tie em up, makes em feel all helpless, but safely. Some girls like that, you know." She sniffed.

"Okay, well, no, Ten, I haven't tried that." The idea wasn't all that strange to him. He knew those games could be fun; after all, hadn't Neela demanded he be less gentle with her?

"Well, maybe you should! Maybe you should try it with me!" Her grin was positively predatory as she reached down and grabbed the hem of her robe.

"Ten, wait a second!" he cried, but it was too late. Her robe was off and over her head.

Dhalius was dumbstruck. He had assumed under the messy, voluminous robes, she would be a spindly, bony creature, like those Goblins he had seen around the city. But Ten was, in a word, voluptuous. Thick thighs led to a small tuft of black and yellow fuzz just under a slightly rounded belly. Her ass had jiggled as she jumped a little to get the robes up and over her heavy breasts, which seemed almost unnaturally large for someone so small in stature, tipped with dark-green nipples. Her skin's yellow stripes reminded him of a tiger, crisscrossing her in jagged lines.

"Come on," she said, tossing her robe to the side and putting a hand on her wide hip. "I know you like the big tits. I've seen you with Korska!" She lifted one mammoth breast and licked her own nipple.

He could try to deny it, but his dick was beginning to strain against his trousers at the sight of her.

"I don't know, Ten," he said, unsure of, well, any of this.

"Yes, you do." She grinned and reached out a hand to grab the tip of his cock, giving it a firm squeeze—it was almost painful but sent a surge of excitement and arousal through him.

"Hey!" he cried, unsure how to respond—part of him was at a loss at how aggressive she was being; part of him *really* liked it.

"Oh, am I bad?" she asked, still holding on to his cock.

"Maybe you should punish me!" she said, feigning a remorseful and sad frown.

"Ten, I would rip you in half," he halfheartedly protested, trying to make her—and himself—see sense.

"Goblins are *very* stretchy." She leaned forward, her mouth inches away from his crotch, grabbed the leather cord keeping his pants up in her teeth, and tugged, untying it and pulling him towards the back of the tent at the same time, her eyes locked on his, filled with devious desire.

"Ten!" he said again, trying to maintain some sort of control of the situation.

"Do you want me to stop?" she asked. "Because I don't think you really want me to." She let go of his straps and tugged his pants down a little, exposing the tip of his cock. Her eyes widened a little, and she bit her lip in excitement.

He reached for her, his heart pounding in his chest from excitement, but she just giggled and danced back out of reached when he tried to grab her. He realized what she was doing.

"You haven't asked me to stop yet," she pointed out in a sing-song voice. "You're enjoying it as much as I am." She darted forward and tugged his pants again, exposing a little more of her prize before retreating again with a mischievous smile.

He was shocked that this woman with whom he had formed this friendship had suddenly turned into this playful but horny brat. She turned away from him and slapped her voluptuous round ass, sending a ripple across the flesh. He reached for her again, but she nimbly dodged under his arm and leapt onto her cot.

She squeezed her breasts together in her hands. "You know you want to get a handful of my handfuls, but you have to earn—" Ten squealed as Dahli's eyes glowed and a tendril of ink wrapped around her ankle and pulled her into the air upside down.

"You were saying?" he asked, stepping forward, but he paused as she reached for him with her hand, staying just out of her reach. She swiped the air, trying to grab his shirt, the mischievous grin still on her face.

"I was saying I want you to restrain me, Sir." Her tongue, unusually long, lolled out of her mouth and licked her full lips.

He laughed a little and finished undoing the pants she had loosened with her teeth, letting them fall to his ankles as he reached down to pull his shirt over his head. While he undressed, the tendrils of ink split and flowed around Ten, wrapping around her ankles, wrists, and throat, tightening enough to hold her still but not hurt her. "I suppose this is a fine method to practice control." He gestured, turning her gently in the air, and brought her closer. He reached up and squeezed her left ass cheek before burying his face in her pussy, his tongue deftly exploring the folds of her sex.

Ten squirmed against the restraints and moaned, arching her back, fighting to break free while pushing her hips against him with a deep moan as he sucked on her clit. He pulled back, his face slick with the juices that ran across her thighs. He spun her in the air and pressed her back against his chest as he reached around to massage her breasts. His fingers found and pinched her nipples lightly, bringing another squeal of delight from the Goblin.

"Are you going to be a good girl for me?" he asked in her ear, running his tongue to the tip, making her shudder.

"Never," she panted, fighting him halfheartedly.

He reached down, enjoying the softness of her ass as he squeezed her, and then gave her a firm slap across her butt cheek. She wiggled a little and stuck her tongue out, blowing a raspberry at him. Encouraged, he spanked her again, harder this time, pulling a gasp and then a giggle from her.

"I need you to be quiet," he said, tightening the ink around her throat just a little.

"Mmmhh, make me," she moaned.

He obliged her, the ink rising from her throat to form

a gag over her mouth. Massaging her breasts once again, he brought two more tendrils of ink up to pry her knees apart, then moved a hand up, exploring her with first one finger and then two, pushing into her vagina, making sure she was ready. Positive that neither of them could wait any longer, he pulled her down onto his waiting cock. He went slowly. No matter what they played, he didn't want to hurt her. But he needn't have bothered. True to her word, her body stretched around him, and from the full-throated moans he could feel reverberating through her, she was loving every inch of him.

He brought her all the way down until she rested nearly against his pelvis. He wrapped one arm around her chest just under her breasts and brought the other one up to wrap his fingers around her throat and provide soft pressure.

"Are you ready, Ten? Are you ready to get what you asked for?"

She looked at him over her shoulder, her eyes rolled back into her skull, and he could feel her smile through the ink as her head rolled in a lazy nod. He dropped both hands to her wide hips to steady himself—the ink would hold her still—and began thrusting up into her. Each time, he would pull out, almost exiting her completely, before slamming back up. Her body shuddered with every move, and he was glad to have gagged her. Her screams rippled through the ink as she bucked against him with all of her strength. He would never have imagined such primal lust from someone so small and kind.

He reached up with one hand, not slowing his thrusts at all, wrapped his fingers in her mane of hair to pull her head back, and gently bit her exposed throat. She whimpered and moved her hips in tight circles in response to his slowed thrusts.

"Oh, you only want to be used, don't you?" he asked. "You want to be punished."

"Mhhmmm!" she agreed with a moan.

He wrapped an arm around her hip and began massaging her labia and clitoris with his hand as he resumed pounding into her as hard and fast as he could. He felt her cum, a sudden flood of slick fluids pulsing around him as she spasmed on his cock. He didn't slow down, giving her no mercy as he fucked her senseless. He realized he was getting close himself.

"Fuck." He gasped. "I'm going to—" He began pulling out, but Ten slammed her head back and glared at him, grinding her ass against him, demanding he finish fucking her.

He banished the ink from around her mouth and pressed his lips to hers as he came, filling her with cum. She moaned into his mouth. Slowly, the moan became a whimper, and she slid back. He used the ink to slowly lift her, his cock falling out of her, followed by a torrent of their combined juices. He set her down on the cot as gently as he could and willed the ink to flow back into the vial he had called it from.

"Gods," he rasped.

"That was so . . . fucking . . . hot!" Ten grinned from the bed. She started to rise but gave up, resting on her side and propping her head up on one hand to gaze at him. "I'm not going to walk right for a week!"

"You are insane; you know that, right?" he asked, reaching for his pants and starting to get dressed.

"You love me," she protested. "Next time, though, we should do it somewhere I can be loud. I like being loud."

"You're always loud," he agreed as he pulled his shirt on. For a moment, he worried this act would taint their friendship, change it in some way, but then he thought of Korska's squad. Yes, they fooled around as often as they felt the need, but it had not poisoned them in any way. "I'm going to run to mess. You want anything?"

"Oh, thank Cra! I'm starving. Oh, and water!" she called as he left the tent.

He moved quickly across the camp to the mess and

grabbed a few left-over pieces of bread from the table—it would be stale, but it would also not be missed—and refilled his water canteen.

"Enjoying yourself?" a voice Dhalius did not know asked from behind him.

He turned and paused, surprised by the sight of another mage.

She stood nearly as tall as him, with porcelain white skin, black hair, and red eyes that seemed to glow in the evening night. She was curvy, stuffed into a black leather corset and spidery skirt that accented her considerable assets and highlighted her figure beautifully. The air around her vibrated with barely restrained power.

"I'm sorry, I don't think we've met. Are you my . . . replacement?" He had known that Captain Lakista had intended to find a female mage as rapidly as possible; he just hadn't expected it to be so quickly, nor had he expected the sudden sadness and despair now that would come with it.

"No. Other way around, actually." She moved past him and picked up a piece of bread. She studied it for a moment before it began to rot in her hand.

A wave of nausea passed through him as her magic passed over his senses.

"What?" he asked, not following, disoriented by the disgusting taste of undeath that stuck cloyingly to the back of his throat. "You're saying I'm your replacement, but that would make you—" He froze.

"Goana, yes." She turned back to him, a cruel smile on her face.

He turned to call for help and realized in terror that the camp was frozen. Women paused mid-step in the distance. The fire stood in time mid-dance. Even the insects and birds of the night were silent, and the stars did not twinkle. He turned back to her, reaching for his spell book, and realized he had left it in Ten's tent and the stave in his own.

"Yes, you are defenseless. Yes, I can kill you. And no, I

can't kill everyone in the camp. Limits to even my power, but only for the moment." She sighed. "But I don't *want* to kill you. I saw your power during that battle with the raiders. You dismantled my toy; you killed my pet. You used the staff," she said, half teasing, half accusing. She stepped past him, trailing a hand across his chest. "I expected a withered old shrew from the Academy, some doddering old fool whose power waned as I waxed. Imagine my surprise when I find a strapping young man." She dropped her hand to the outline of his penis. He jerked back from her touch.

"Oh, don't be like that. I know you're fucking some of these lost causes; I can smell the cum and pussy on you." She leaned close and sniffed like a dog. "It's intoxicating. But you could be fucking all of them. You could be a prince, a king, a god by my side. Imagine . . . you could be fucking me and all of them, whenever and however you wanted." She stepped back and spread her arms. "Bring me the stave, and I will enslave the world for your pleasure."

"You will enslave nothing. We will stop you," Dhalius growled, surprised how much he hated this foul woman.

"If they are employing a man, a young, witless man who can't even see the value of what I offer, they are truly desperate." She laughed. "Tell the Lakista sisters that I am thinking of them, and that I look forward to using their hollowed skulls to sip my wine from."

"I'll tell them only that you await our sword!" he shouted back, but she was gone.

The camp had sprung back to life in an instant and several women had turned to look at him as though he were insane. He ignored them, rushing off to find the captain once more.

Allegiance to the Host

D HALI PUSHED HIS way into the command tent and froze. In front of him, Lakista and her lieutenants stood speaking to the same Guild official whom he had traveled with weeks ago, Geoffrey Dennen. He was flanked by two Guild guards; everyone looked on edge.

"Master Dennen?" he asked, looking between the four.

"Master Dennen has arrived to inform me they have a sorceress that can meet our needs, one who can replace you," Captain Lakista said, her fierce eyes not leaving Geoffrey's.

"I . . . see," he said slowly, his heart dropping. He took a deep breath. "Before you dismiss me, I—"

"You are not dismissed," Lieutenant Jaxsi snapped from her place beside Lakista.

"What?" Dhali asked

"Easy, Jaxsi," Lakista said.

"I will not be easy! We are not some kingdom-funded army. We are not a lackey service to be commanded and reprimanded at will, especially not by some old fat man."

"Careful, creature," Dennen warned, his tone cruel and flat. It was a side of him Dhali had not seen before.

"You will treat my staff with respect, Guild-man," Lakista warned. "She is twice the warrior those soldiers of yours are, literally and figuratively. As I said, Dhalius is one of us now. He is going nowhere unless he decides to take his leave. We have a Guild charter, but we are our own mercenary company; we are free women who do and accept who we please."

"You demanded I find—" Dennen started.

"And you denied my demands, Dennen. I am growing tired of this dance." The contrast to the conversation before, when Dennen had forced Dhalius on her, was staggering. She would not be put wrong-footed this time.

"His sisters' company has specifically requested he join them. Would you separate his family? Deny his own wishes?"

"His wishes?" she said as though the thought just occurred to her. "That is a splendid idea, Dennen. Mage, come here." He stepped forward past Dennen's guards to stand beside the Guild-man. Lakista watched him like a cat watching an injured mouse, knowing it has nowhere to run. "You know your options. You are a free soldier and mage. Do you wish to go serve with their company instead?"

Dhalius swallowed. He looked at Dennen, who shot him an angry warning look, a look that promised he would make Dhali's life hell if he needed to. Dhali pushed his feet together and stood straight, preserving as much dignity as his half-dressed state would allow. "While I would love to serve alongside my sisters, my place is with the Defiant Host now until I am incapable of serving!" he barked.

"There you have it, Dennen. He's made his choice. You may tell his sisters that they are welcome here; we'll find stations for them if they decide they wish it." She waved her hand, dismissing the man.

"You're a bitch, Lakista. It is unwise to make an enemy of the Guild," Dennen hissed.

"You're wasting your breath. We are the Defiant Host, we let our record speak for us, and our record shines like sterling *with* Dhalius in our midst. Get. Out."

As soon as Dennen had left the tent, Dhalius stepped forward. "Captain . . . thank you."

Lakista looked up and nodded. "You've proven yourself. You've been loyal, obedient, and a hard worker. That is all I ask of my mercs. Well, that and being the best there is." Her staff chuckled as they moved back to their own desks. "There was something you wished to say, I assume?"

"Yes!" He realized he had been so caught up in the relief at Lakista's decision to keep him that he had almost forgotten the dire portents of his evening.

"Goana . . . " he said. Every eye turned towards him. "Goana came to me, in the camp."

He went over the details of his encounter as best he could remember, detailing the threats and the implications of godhood once more. When he was done, he exhaled and waited for Lakista's furious reaction.

"Why are you alive? Why are any of us? If she can freeze time and traipse in here?" Jaxsi asked.

"She can't," Dhalius said, his mind turning around that same problem. "Time magic is . . . strange, and difficult. It is . . . much easier to affect an individual than an area, especially to manipulate their awareness. I don't think she was actually here. She was just pushing some sort of vision onto me."

"That isn't comforting, Dhalius," the other lieutenant—a serpentine Naga named Sharami—said, crossing her arms over her human torso as she sat on her coils. "How did she even know about you, and how do we make sure she doesn't somehow drive you mad and use you as a weapon?"

"I think she traced the energy from the Staff of Viscu. I used it in the battle. She must have been watching, tasted the magic, and followed it here." He shook his head. "There are limits, something she is lacking; she was attempting to win me to her cause."

"What did she offer you?" Lakista asked.

"Well . . . the Host," he said softly.

"What? She wanted to give you my position?" Lakista chuckled.

"No, Captain, she wanted to make you my . . . concubine slaves." He swallowed his tongue, looking down, ready once again for the fury of his captain. Instead, he was shocked as all three women began laughing, Lakista hardest of all, nearly falling out of her seat.

"I'm sorry, you're saying she thought she could, what? Find you *more* green women to bed?" she barked.

Dhalius felt the blush starting at the tips of his ears and traveling down his neck until his entire chest was beet red. "You knew?" he asked.

"Why do you think I knew with such certainty you would not accept Dennen's offer? Don't insult me, mage. It is my duty to know everything that could affect the morale and cohesion of my outfit. Did you really think your little romps with Squad Korska were a mystery? Why do you think I had you join their unit permanently? Or maybe you thought no one knew that you and Ten disappeared into each other's tents every night for hours at a time."

He was about to argue that they had just been studying all this time but then remembered his half-dressed state, and the reason for it, and shut his mouth. "Master Joachima said that it wasn't an issue."

"And it isn't. It's just funny that Goana thinks because no one wants to bed her that no one else is fucking. It is a sign of their own ineptitude that each time it comes to trying to corrupt you, they try to appeal to your lust." She sighed a little, her mirth subsiding. "But the concern remains. If she can get in your head, how can we protect us from you or you from her?"

Dhalius squirmed a little. He had an answer for that too, but he wasn't a fan of it. "There is one way."

"Well?" Jaxsi asked. "Spit it out."

"Is there a tattooist in the company?" he asked.

It was halfway through the camp, being marched by Jaxsi, that he realized he had never brought Ten her water or food. He hoped the Goblin would forgive him as he stuck his head into her tent. Luckily, she was bundled up, back in her robes, snoring peacefully on her cot. He snuck in and grabbed his ink and books and emerged a second later.

"It's late, and this will be meticulous work. Maybe we should wait until morning," he whispered.

"Every second you are unprotected is another second that she could enter your mind," Jaxsi said. "You don't need to fear; many members of the Host have ink. It's going to be fine."

He had seen tattoos go very wrong. Infection could tear a man's body and skin apart, and that was before you considered the arcane nature of what he had in mind. He had seen the wards in the Academy where the insane, driven mad by their own arcane ink, were kept. In seeking power, they had lost everything. Scribes were the most prone to this hubris, and the most likely to fall.

But Jaxsi was right. It would not matter if he was sane or not if Goana could reach into his thoughts and manipulate his senses. It made him a threat to everyone around him, including—no—especially his squad. He steeled himself.

"You're right. I'm ready."

Jaxsi led him through the camp once more, only stopping at a medium-sized red yurt at the edge of the camp. From inside, he could hear the dulcet tones of some stringed instrument he didn't recognize, and a haze of smoke filtered out from inside.

"Eloni?" Jaxsi called from outside. "You have a customer."

The music stopped for a second, and then a thickly accented voice called back. "Come in."

Jaxsi lifted the tent flap, allowing a cloud of smoke to escape. It was thick and heavily scented—incense, Dhalius realized. He steadied his nerves and pushed through the cloud to enter the tent.

Inside, it was like he had stepped into another world.

Carpets, pillows, and tapestries covered every surface. In one corner of the room, a slight and heavily tattooed Wood Elf played a guzheng. Several chains hanging from the roof of the yurt lazily exuded incense smoke that made his head swim pleasantly. But most surprising was the woman who rose to meet them. He had never met one of the Arachians before, but there was no mistaking what this woman was.

She was charcoal black with swirling white tattoos covering almost every visible inch of exposed skin. And while fully dressed, her two sets of arms allowed for more exposed skin than most would show. Her face was beautiful and angular, but in addition to two larger almond-shaped eyes, a number of smaller round eyes dotted the left side of her face, each with a different shaped pupil. Her hands, each with three fingers, ended in small talons. She wore a modified kimono, a garment from a faraway kingdom he had only ever read about. While her face was undoubtedly feminine, her body—from what he could see—lacked any secondary sexual traits, much like Tawna or other nonmammalian members of the company.

The Arachian race was secretive and rarely left the jade forests of their homelands. He had never thought to meet one. When traveling, they often bundled in so many layers of fabric that they were impossible to identify, and he knew next to nothing about their culture. He knew they were proud hunters, famed artisans, and he knew their mouths hid large, flexible fangs that could inject a terrifying poison that caused flesh and organs to liquefy. He had heard tales that they were not picky about their prey, and rumors of cannibalism abounded.

On top of that, Wood Elves also had a primal reputation. They considered cannibalizing their enemies to be the highest honor you could pay a fallen foe. Of course, these were just rumors, and in the polite societies of Estherfel, cannibalism and the consumption of any intelligent race was strictly forbidden.

His nerves came crashing back.

"It is late, friend Jaxsi," the Arachian, who must have been Eloni, said softly.

"I know you prefer late nights, Mistress Eloni," Jaxsi said with a deep bow.

"That I do," Eloni responded with a slight nod, several of her eyes sliding to Dhalius. "This is my subject? My canvas?"

"It is, and this is a special case, Mistress. The company will be paying you for this work."

"Lucky man." Eloni breathed it out. "I am not cheap," she explained.

Jaxsi nodded. "Take it from here. Dhalius, come see the captain when it is done, or in the morning, whichever comes later." With that, she left, leaving him in the care of the two predatory women.

He watched her go and then turned back to Eloni "I need protective tattoos using a special ink," he explained, and set his books down to find the appropriate pages.

"You are a scribe, yes?" Eloni asked, kneeling next to him to watch as he turned the pages of his books.

"Oh, yes. I am, sorry," he said, realizing he had been rude to this potentially deadly woman who would soon hold his life and sanity in her hands. "My name is Dhalius. It . . . is good to meet you, Mistress Eloni."

"Others have spoken of you, mixed opinions, mixed feelings," she said, tracing the symbol on the page he had landed on. She rose and moved around him as if studying an unfinished painting. "You do not know how lucky you are, friend Dhalius." She offered a small grin.

He felt her hands on his shoulders, guiding him down to prop him up on a cushion. He didn't know if her strength came naturally or if his senses and will were being sapped by the heady scent of the perfumed smoke.

"How so?" he asked, his stomach twisting in knots, knowing he was fully at the mercy of this alien being.

"You do not know the full history; it isn't taught. Human supremacy clouds the truth like a fog hides the ambush. Atramentomancy was crafted by my people. We did not call it this; the word would not sit well in your human mouth, but it amounted to Ink-Weaving in your tongue, if you abandon nuance." Despite her words, there was no judgment in her tone. She gathered a few things from a shelf on the far side of her yurt and returned to kneel next to him again, gently taking the vial of ink from him. In her hand, she held several short wooden rods and a number of small bone implements.

"How did you come to join the Host?" he asked, hoping to delay the coming pain.

She spoke as she poured small amounts of his ink into a thimble-sized glass cup. "I did not join. I travel with the Host, and their number come to me for decoration. I give small discounts, and I provide stories for their fire. I travel with them so that I may be safe as I travel this world, exploring it, tasting the experiences it has to offer." She brought his books closer, flipping through several, though she left the page showing the ward he needed open. "This is an old language, but you are worried of an attack to your mind?" she asked.

"Yes, a mage named Goana invaded my senses earlier this evening. Truth be told, I don't want to do this, but I cannot take the risk of vulnerability," he said softly. "It puts everyone at risk, and I won't be responsible for the deaths of my friends."

"That is a burden all soldiers take on, Dhalius, if you fail in battle, if you falter. But it is a nice aspiration, and it is good that you do as you can." She clicked her tongue, and the music stopped. A moment later, the Wood Elf appeared in his periphery. She was holding a razor.

"What!?" Dhalius exclaimed, trying to rise, but Eloni held him down.

"We must shave the areas we are to tattoo. Calm yourself; it would not do to nick you before we work." With her hand on his chest to keep him still, the Elf crouched over him and got to work.

DECORATED SOLDIER

I T WAS LATE morning before Dhalius emerged from Eloni's yurt, stumbling a little from exhaustion. His skin ached, and the warm morning air stung the fresh ink. He was in a daze, made hazy by the inhalation of the smoke. He drew quite a few stares as he moved towards the mess hall. Eloni had ordered he drink as much water as he could hold and then get into the shade. To be honest, all he wanted was to sleep, but he had been ordered to return to the captain.

"Dhali?" He turned and saw Henrietta. Her mouth fell open, and she grinned up at him. "Ah, you spent the night at the spinner! You finally look like a real man. Well, still missing a beard . . . "

It took his pain- and smoke-addle brain a few moments to remember that getting tattooed was a rite of passage into adulthood for her people.

"I thought I had proven myself man enough," he said slowly, trying to focus his thoughts.

Henri blushed at that and grinned, the bashful smile that played across her lips quite fetching. "Well, mebbe so . . . but lemme see ye!" She walked around him, scrutinizing his red angry skin. "A little fancy, in my opinion," she said, eying him up and down. "And that is a lot for your first."

He nodded. He had intended Eloni to just tattoo the wards necessary for protection, but in the deep trance he had been put in, Eloni had kept going, seemingly immune to fatigue. Now arcane symbols traced their way from the back of his skull down the right of side of his neck, pec, and ribs. He raised his right arm, seeing the spider scrawl of runes and sigils that covered him from shoulder to the first knuckle on his hands. She had, in his opinion, gone overboard. Somewhere in the back of his mind, he worried about the cost that would be levied for the hours of work.

Finally, he found his voice. "It is to protect and hone my magic," he said hoarsely and started walking again towards the mess to get his water. "I was attacked last night."

"Wait, ye were attacked?!" she exclaimed, rushing to fall in beside him, her hand, wider and larger than his, grabbing his undecorated hand and squeezing it gently.

"Magical attack against my brain." He raised a finger and tapped his skull. "Had to protect it, had to protect my squad from it, from me." He sighed. "I'm sorry, Henri, I'm having trouble thinking straight. I have not yet slept. I'm getting some water, then reporting to the captain. I'll catch up with you at drills, yes?"

Henri frowned but nodded, and then smiled and dropped his hand. "Take care, Dhali. I'll let Korska and the others know!" And with that, she marched off on her own errands.

Dhalius watched her go, warmed by both her concern and his own affection for the powerful warrior, and turned back to his own tasks. Being out of the tent was clearing his head. The more fresh air he took in, the more his thoughts became unmuddled. Unfortunately, with that clarity came the pain. He hurried to get water, waving off greetings and calls from those who were surprised at his new decor, and then hurried back to the command tent. He pushed his way inside once more and stood in the entry, waiting to be acknowledged.

"Mage, come in," Lakista called from her desk.

He approached and then stood still, once again waiting for her to give him her attention. Neela stood next to the captain, and he offered her a smile—as best he could through the pain and exhaustion. She met his eyes, that cold, indifferent stare of hers making him self-conscious, before she spoke.

"Dhalius. It is good to see you. You hurt? Can I soothe your pain?" she asked, stepping around the desk.

"Neela, I would welcome it," he said. "But I don't know how the spells will react to your magic yet. We should be—" He was going to say *careful*, but she was already touching his chest, her power flowing into him like a soothing balm. His pain evaporated under her attention like fog in the morning sun. He sighed in relief. "Gods, thank you," he whispered.

"Of course," she said, returning to Lakista's side. "Those are wounds, Dhalius, decorative wounds, but wounds nonetheless. Report to the medical tent each evening until they are fully healed. I will not have you dying of sepsis. And stay out of the river. Wash using a rag, not through swimming."

"Yes, Neela." He nodded.

"I like your new look. It is fetching. I also like that she worked in the company crest. You are ours now forever." Her flat tone almost made him miss the compliment, and then he was so pleased to hear her kindness he almost missed the comment of the crest.

"What?" He craned his neck to try to get a look at every inch of his skin.

"Upper right chest," the captain said without looking up from her work. "I sent a messenger to suggest it. Apparently, both you and Eloni liked the idea. There is a mirror in the corner if you wish to see for yourself."

Dhali wasn't sure how to feel about being marked as property of the company but moved to look in the mirror as directed. Indeed, just below his collarbone and above his nipple sat the crest of the Defiant Host, featuring a stylized wyvern smashing an army under one foot and breaking a sword with its other claw, its wings forming a shield and making it appear as a coat of arms. It was intricate and flowed into the arcane symbols beautifully. He moved a little, watching the way the enchanted ink seemed to shimmer slightly as the light caught it.

"Enough preening," Lakista ordered. Mollified, he returned to her desk. She finally looked up at him and nodded. "How do you feel?" she asked.

"Like I've fallen off a horse and been dragged for a kilometer," he answered truthfully. "But right now, I just want to go back to my tent and sleep."

"Right." She leaned back in her chair and thought for a moment. "Granted, but as soon as you're recovered enough, we need to discuss our defenses and our plan of attack. The next battle with the Eaves will undoubtedly be heavy on the magic side. I need you practiced and ready to perform. You've studied tactics?"

"Yes, Captain, at the Academy."

"Good. I want you training with our healers and clerics. They have a wide range of defensive magic at their disposal. Make sure they are ready, and they will do the same for you. Ten-Tulips said you were concerned about live practice."

Dhalius blushed again, remembering how that conversation had ended with Ten, but just nodded. "Yes, Captain."

"Good. Neela, see the mage back to his tent." She looked back down at the maps and missives on her desk. Neela stepped back around the desk and towards Dhali. "And, Neela, just that. No feeding. The boy needs his rest."

Neela shot the captain a look but nodded and took Dhalius's uninjured arm in her elbow and walked him out.

"I am not used to everything I do being under scrutiny," he grumbled, exasperated by the lack of privacy.

"We are close-knit, Dhalius. Word and sounds travel fast," Neela said calmly.

"I suppose," he accepted begrudgingly. "Though having the captain's eyes on my personal life does make me a bit nervous."

"My sister attempts to keep her eyes on everything," Neela said. "But is especially attentive to me and, of course, you as an anomaly in the company. You should feel honored that she suggested you get the company's seal. She would not do so if she did not believe you belonged."

"Wait," Dhalius whispered, as though what was being said was a conspiracy needing to be hidden. "*Sister? You are the captain's sister?*"

"Yes. I am Neela Lakista. Tori is my sister."

He ignored the use of the captain's given name; it made her seem less mythic in a way, more . . . human. "But you aren't human, and she is . . . How . . . Oh, you were adopted by her—" Dhalius said, his mind working to figure out what seemed to be impossible.

"No, by blood, or by birth, I suppose. Our father was hanged for various crimes when she was young. I was born from his . . . leavings." She glanced up thoughtfully. "I suppose I was adopted by our mother, though. In this way, you are right." She paused outside his tent and turned to face him.

"Neela, why haven't you visited, since . . . ?"

"Because you and I have both been busy." He tried to read her, but her empty, bored gaze held no answers for him. "But when I have time, I would visit again."

"You are welcome to. I . . . thought I had offended you, or—" He shrugged. "I missed your company."

She looked at him oddly, the same look she had given him when he suggested she spend the night. "You missed watering me," she corrected. "Which is odd, considering the frequency you have been—"

"Okay, I understand," he said, holding up a hand to stop her from going further.

She smirked, a small glint of warmth reaching her eyes. "I will see you this evening in the medical tent. Good day, Dhalius." And with that, she turned and made her way back through the camp.

He watched her for a moment before he pushed into

his small tent, fell into his cot, and, within moments, was snoring gently.

When he woke, Dhalius was surprised to find he wasn't alone. Sitting up, he groaned and looked at his squad and Ten, who all sat arrayed around him in a half circle, chatting and sharing their noon meal. Ten noticed him sitting up first.

"Way to leave a girl hanging," she said with a smile.

"Sorry, something came up," he said, a wry grin on his face.

"We know. Captain Lakista filled me in during morning briefings," Korska said "Now stand up; let us get a look at the new Dhalius."

He slowly stood and turned his body to the women, appreciating their oohs and aahs.

"Gotta admit, you weren't hard to look at before, better now." Korska chuckled. "Look more like a shaman than a mage, though. We'll make an Orc out of you yet."

"Nah, he's gonna be a Dwarven stone speaker, just got get momma's approval, then I'll get him a dowry and wed him up." Henri glanced around at the women, who were staring at her trying to determine if she was joking. "What? I'll still share. I'm nice like that!"

"I'm jealous," Tawna said from the corner, sitting back on her haunches.

"You want to marry him too?" Korska asked, laughing.

"No, of the decorations," she hissed in annoyance.

"Why? You want someone to poke you with needles for hours on end?" Dhali asked.

"Well no, but even if I were to want so, my scales would not allow it." She shrugged. "But it does suit you."

"Thank you, Tawna," he said. "What time is it?"

"Just after noon-mess. We wouldn't have let ye sleep through drills. Momma says that ye need to get over yourself and get back to work, by the way. I think that's her way of saying she is worried," Henri said. "She also said we need to let ye rest and recover your stamina for a minute."

"Gods, is there anyone in the camp that isn't informed about my sex life?" he lamented.

"Maybe stop fucking everything that moves?" Ten suggested, and then laughed when he glared at her. "I would rather you *didn't*, though." She rose, stretching. "I have to get back to my own work. The captain has me making the fun stuff."

"Fun stuff?" Gisla asked.

Ten turned back, her smile growing terrifyingly wicked. "Bombs." She cupped her hands in front of her, mimicking an explosion in micro. "Boooom," she whispered before heading out the flap.

Korska shook her head. "She's terrifying."

"I prefer the company of terrifying women, Korska. Why do you think I like you all so much?" He grinned as he sat and found himself some fresh clothes, swiftly changing and doing a few light stretches to work the stiffness out of his joints.

"Because you're a horny idiot?" Gisla suggested.

"Thank you for that, Gisla." He chuckled and nodded. "Okay." He grabbed a small leather bandolier and set a few vials of ink in it. In battle, he could wear his robes and bring his spell book, but he didn't want to deplete his grimoire before he actually needed it. "Shall we?"

The five of them pushed out of his tent. He wondered how one could acquire one of the larger tents in the future. It might have to do with rank. He had yet to see inside anyone's but his, Ten's, and Eloni's tent so far, and technically speaking, Eloni wasn't even a member of the company.

They walked through the camp to the training grounds where the Naga was leading drills, maintaining the combat efficiency of the company ten squads at a time. When she saw the squad, she broke away and informed them to continue on into the field, where they would meet the Elves and the clerics for their new training regimen.

It was strange, actually—for weeks he had traveled, trained, and fought with the Defiant Host, yet this was the first time he was truly meeting other magic-users, other than Neela or Ten. He felt them as he approached, an entire squad of women versed in the mystic arts. The energy they gave off washed over him. It was hard to explain to nonpractitioners, but it was like a flavored pressure building in his skull. Nearly any mage could not only identify other wizards and sorceresses but also guess at their school of magic. While holy mysticism was its own thing, it was a kind of magic nonetheless, and he could taste the multitudes of their power.

He also knew some of them were lying. He was considered a battle mage but could easily be fielded in a defensive capacity. Two of the women before him were Elementalists; he could taste the cold chill of ice magic and the musty odor of stone magic on them. Even if they were clerics of nature deities, they should be able to give as good as they got. But for whatever reason, they had decided not to use these two to fulfill the obligation to field a battle mage. It might be their own preference, but with how much Lakista had detested the idea of him joining, how she had even suggested they needed no mage at all, it made him think she did not *know* the extent of the power of her own clerics. And for a woman who prided herself in understanding her company in full, that made no sense.

That left only a few possibilities, such as them lying about their abilities, though he could think of no beneficent reason to do so. He shook the thoughts from his head. There was a far simpler explanation—they simply had never trained in offensive spellwork. Each magic-user trod their own path; it was not his to question another caster on the why's or how's. And with his own arcane tattoos and the sinister reputation of his own school of sorcery, they would likely have misgivings about him as well.

Now that he had realized that, it felt idiotic that he had not sought them out before this. He bowed deeply as they approached. "Hello. I am Dhalius LeReux, adapt of the school of—"

"No need to be so formal, Dhalius LeReux. We all know who you are. I am Estefani, and this is my squad. I was surprised when you were assigned to Korska, but . . . " The woman's hazel eyes slid over to the warriors who accompanied Dhali. "I understand that you formed a kinship during your first battle with the Host. These things are hard to overcome. Still, we have been expecting you to join us in the Sanctum tent long before this."

"Sanctum tent?" Dhali said, feeling even more foolish now. Of *course* there was a sanctum tent, a place where the magic-users of the company would gather to conduct their studies. It would be a combination of holy place, traveling library, and workshop. "I've been preparing my spells and studying with Ten-Tulips," he admitted.

"The *Goblin*?" one of the women asked, a look of disdain on her face. Dhali decided he deeply disliked the woman then and there.

"The alchemist, and yes, she is a Goblin," he said, a bit of edge to his voice. He felt Korska touch his shoulder and had to remind himself that only a few weeks ago, he had held his own prejudices and assumptions about not just the Goblin race but about Orc kind as well. If not for them seeking him out to befriend him, he might well have the same reaction. He swallowed his ire.

"She is a good friend and an excellent alchemist," he said. "I will have to start joining you all in the Sanctum tent, though," he lied. "It will be good to share thoughts and studies with other users of the mystic and arcane arts. But for now, we should figure out how to fight cohesively together." He nodded to Korska and then to Palaas, who had stood by in silence watching the exchange to ensure they were ready.

He reached down to pull the Staff of Viscu from his belt. He had spent long hours refining the work that Ten had done initially, treating the hairs and shaping them until he could use it as an actual calligraphy brush. Hours more pulling the ink from the pages of his spellbook and reapplying them with the brush. It was courtship between him and the holy artifact. He didn't know whether it would be enough, but it was all he could do. The voices still sang to him, urging him on to acts both profane and holy. The staff wanted to be made whole, and it wanted to unleash its full potential. But now it was more of a conversation instead of them screaming in his skull demanding his obedience. Many men and women had fallen to the will of powerful artifacts, becoming more or less thralls in the service of long dead consciousnesses. Dhalius was determined not to join their number.

He spun the brush expertly in his hand as though it were a short sword and looked up at the clerics. "Shall we begin?"

SHOWING RESTRAINT

DHALIUS ROLLED BACK, barely avoiding the melon-sized chunk of ice that whizzed past his head. As he rose, he spun his brush around and brought an arc of ink through the air towards the approaching circle of sorceresses. It slammed against a shield of stone and was deflected. He spun again, recalling the ink so as to not waste the precious resource. As he did, something snagged his leg, breaking his concentration. He looked down and saw a vine had grown and wrapped around him. A moment later, he was dangling in the air as the vine ripped him up and off his feet.

Korska charged in, slicing through the vine with an axe, while Tawna and Henrietta deflected the rain of tar-tipped arrows the rangers fired at them. Korska helped him to his feet, and he nodded his thanks before turning back to the clerics. Or at least, where he knew they were. One of them had summoned a thick fog, obscuring the casters from view.

"Have a plan, Dhali?" Korska asked, ducking behind Henri's shield.

"Maybe. You and Tawna distract the rangers. Henri, keep me from getting an arrow to the knee. Gisla, I'm going to charge the others, but I want you to take on the ice maiden."

"Charge? You're a fucking mage," Henri growled.

"Which is why it will work," he explained. "Go!"

When it came to magic, there were few things more

misunderstood than a magic duel. Most pictured mages throwing fireballs at one another, countering spells and then responding in kind. The truth was by the time your foe cast a spell, it was far too late to attempt to counter it yourself. Much like in swordplay, if you waited until the blade was at your throat, you could no longer hope to parry.

Others likened it to a chess match, thoughtful plays as you attempted to outthink your opponent—after all, were magic-users not incredibly clever strategists and tacticians? This, of course, was bullshit as well. It was immensely difficult to form any sort of strategy while someone was lobbing giant balls of acid in your direction. That, and most mages were more than a bit cloud-headed, thoughts too scattered to mount a good offense despite years of academic training.

No, a magic duel was a frantic melee often decided by three factors. Whose magic was most powerful, whose magic was most flexible, and whose use of magic was most creative. In larger-scaled battles, two other factors came into play. The first was control—the mage with the best control of their power would do the least damage to their own army. And the mage with the best army could be backed up by their squad.

Dhalius rushed forward, trusting Henri to keep up with him. Korska and Tawna split off at the same time, Tawna's hard scales and shield deflecting arrows in equal measure as she closed the distance with the Elves. Korska wasn't nearly as fast as the rangers, but she sheathed her axe and grabbed the long-chained chigiriki-jutsu she kept coiled at her hip and, with a whip of her arm, sent the iron ball flying across the practice grounds. The Elves scattered, unable to keep cohesion in the face of the Orc's crushing weapon.

Dhalius summoned more ink from one of his vials—he was running low; this was his last gambit to end the fight before he was effectively hobbled. He formed the ink into a long-hafted warhammer forming up and from the brush.

All the destructive power of the weapon with none of the weight. He spun and slammed his summoned weapon into the earthen shield that had formed as they approached, powdering stone into sand. All he needed was an opening. He slipped in, jumping and rolling through the gap he created in the other mystic's shield, and rose in the middle of their formation. He kicked out, planting his boot against the back of the stone-cleric, and pushed her into the very wall of earth she had formed. She was staggered, but a shimmering shield of energy formed around her to protect her from more harm.

Dhalius spun, dropping to use the hammer to yank the offending cleric who had summoned the protective aura off her feet. Rising in one smooth motion, he raised the hammer above his head.

"Enough! You've lost this!" Estefani suddenly shouted, rage writ on her face.

"Have I?" he asked.

As the chaos of the battle cleared and the spells dissipated around them, the truth was revealed. Tawna and Korska had scattered the Elves. They had taken plenty of wounds, but none of them looked lethal from where Dhalius stood. Four clerics had turned toward Dhalius, four hands pointed at him, ready to unleash their gods' might to tear the foolish man apart. Henri was panting, winded from trying to pound her way through their spells. Dhalius pointed. A few meters away, Gisla stood, her blunted dagger to the ice-cleric's throat, her other hand around her mouth.

"Your circle is broken," he said. "One by one, you all would have been picked off."

"You would have died if this were a real fight," Estefani spat.

"Maybe, but my squad would have ended yours. Maybe I would have lost this fight, but we would have won the battle."

"You cheated! This was to be a magic battle, not some

ham-fisted melee brawl!" the ice-cleric shouted as Gisla released her.

"Cheated?" Korska laughed as she walked up. "You expect our enemies to play fair? You lost a training exercise. Why are you so bent out of shape over it?"

"Because," Dhalius said, meeting Estefani's eyes, "they didn't expect to. They never have before because Goana did not push them to excel so it would be easier to betray them." A heavy silence hung over all of their heads at his words. "She wanted you ill prepared for a trained battle mage. She wanted you to be overconfident. I don't want to beat you; I want you to beat me. I want you to turn away every possible attack I can throw at you, because in a *real* fight? You are protecting *me*; you are protecting all of us. I will never go easy on any of you because I can feel how powerful you all are and how much more powerful you can all be."

Estefani held his gaze, her anger giving away to shame. She broke the stare first.

"You should not sacrifice your squad for victory," Palaas said as the Elves approached. "It was a good tactic to stop the holy-ones, but in the end, they would have been felled."

"Lucky for us, in a real fight, the best rangers are on our side, but noted," Dhalius said. "I'm not the best either. I failed in protecting all of us. But that's why we train, yes? Not for idle practice and to feel good about ourselves."

"Right." Korska nodded. "We do so to discover where we are weak and address it."

"Before we are in a real fight," Henri finished.

Dhalius nodded and offered his hand to Estefani. "Shall we go again?"

She stared at him, her frustration at losing and at his words warring across her face. After a long moment, her anger gave way to a grim determination. She nodded but did not take his hand. "Yes, but this time, we get Korska's squad, and you fight with the Elves."

The rest of training had gone as smoothly as it could with the general animosity between the parties. He got the impression that the Elves simply felt they were *better* than anyone else. It didn't actually matter that he was human or a man; it only mattered that he was *not* an Elf. He wondered how they took orders from the captain with that stuffy attitude. He had realized that, when working with them, he could not issue any suggestions or orders, as they would simply be ignored or overridden. Instead, he had worked to defend them from his squad while they tried to whittle their way through the shields and defensive magic of the clerics.

The clerics. Gods, after that first loss, they had grown aggressive, trying to prove Dhalius wrong, or at least prove they could defeat him. And they certainly could, but an angry caster was a caster that had already lost control. Dhalius could see the cracks in their armor. Where before they had been overconfident, they had become too emotional. He understood all too well; it was a difficult needle to thread. In the end, he had had to concede, as he had run out of ink and could no longer effectively use his own magic, the limitations of his own craft painfully evident. What would he do in a prolonged engagement?

Dhalius had gone and washed off—as Neela commanded, using only a rag and a bucket of water. He grabbed food from the mess and then headed to the medical tent. Neela soothed his aches, complaining about the amount of dirt that had obviously gotten on his skin. "You are not an Alarune; you don't need soil to grow," she had admonished him before seeing to his health, and then dismissed him. He had stopped by to ask Ten to craft more ink for him, hoping she wasn't getting tired of his constant need for supply, and then finally retired to his own tent for the night.

It had felt good to get out and actually sling spells. There had been a tension, sure, but to actually be practicing the craft, improving, felt great. There was also something about working with other mystic practitioners that was different. There was an intimacy involved in spellwork that was nearly impossible to describe to someone who had never, and likely would never, experience it. And while he wouldn't tell a soul this, it was *different* now. He had felt his spellwork, and theirs, in his veins. The tattoos he now wore absorbed that power. He could feel it washing through him, allowing him greater stores of energy and a greater understanding of the clerics' abilities and of his own.

Lighting a candle in his tent, Dhalius rolled up his sleeve and turned his hand over, observing the way his tattoos caught and reflected the light. He knew his mother would be horrified. He smirked, thinking of her reaction. *Dhalius!* she would say. *Tattoos are for pirates and thieves! Not for upstanding young men!* But here he was, almost as much tattoo as he was man at this juncture.

"Do you spend much time staring at yourself, human?"

Dhalius spun, startled by the presence in his tent. He had not heard or felt anyone enter, and after Goana's attack, he was terrified of assassins. There, leaning against his trunk, stood Palaas. She wore a mask of indifferent annoyance, but he was almost sure that was just the natural expression of Elven kind at this point.

"Only when it's so different than I am used to," he said.

"In the field and in training," Palaas began, studying her own fingernails as though everything else in the tent was unworthy of her attention, "do not think to order me or my rangers around like common milk maids."

"I would never treat any of you with such—"

"Or at all," she finished, her eyes flicking up in annoyance.

"Right." He closed his eyes and rubbed them with the tips of his fingers. "I apologize, Palaas."

"Mistress," she corrected.

"Excuse me?" he asked, opening his eyes to stare at her. She met his gaze unwaveringly, not an ounce of humor in the look.

"I have a title. Use it. Mistress." She sneered.

"Very well, I apologize, *Mistress* Palaas," he said with a slight bow.

"Good boy," she said, cocking her head as though she were congratulating a flea-bitten mutt on learning to not soil itself.

"You trained at the Academy?" she asked. "To learn tactics and how to work as a unit?"

"Yes, but," he began, then corrected himself when she shot him a sharp look. "Yes, *Mistress.*" It was reminding him of some of his more strict instructors. "But the majority of my learning came from working with my sisters' company and their battle mage. Experience is a better teacher than books."

"Why didn't you join them?" she asked.

"I tried. The Guild sent me here, and now . . . well, I like it here, and the captain branded me, so I suppose I'm here to stay . . . Mistress."

She didn't respond, staring at him with her cold sapphire eyes, inhumanly still. If she had not been speaking a moment ago, he could have been convinced she was a statue. He shuffled a little, wondering why the Elf was suddenly so interested in the ins and outs of who he was, and why she now stood in silence staring.

"Hmph," she huffed, breaking the stalemate, and gestured at his cot with the back of her hand. "Lay down," she ordered and reached town to begin untying her trousers.

"Excuse me?" he asked. He understood the order, and the action, but her tone and attitude made him doubt. "Why?"

"Why, *Mistress,*" she corrected. "Because I want a place to sit in this filthy hovel you call a tent, and I have chosen your face." She finished untying the leather strap and pushed her pants down to her ankles, then rose and kicked them off.

He stared at her. As horrid a bitch as she could be, she *was* remarkably beautiful, at least what he could see. She was almost a complete opposite of Ten, long and lithe with no trace of body fat to her. Her vagina looked soft and inviting, dew drops of moisture dotting her thighs giving lie to her disinterest. Soft blond pubic hair was trimmed into an elegant design. He decided not to question further and began working at the ties of his own pants.

"Stop. Did I say I wanted to see your disgusting . . . phallus?" she snapped.

Dhalius froze and looked up again, confused. Slowly, he sat on the edge of his cot and lay down facing her. She approached and, staring down at him, used her knee to push his shoulder until he was lying flat on his back. She placed her knee to the side of his head and brought her other knee up so she was kneeling on his cot with his face between her thighs, then she lowered herself, pushing her sex against his mouth.

Dhalius eagerly accepted kissing her labia majora before slowly licking across her lips. His eyes widened as he recognized the taste—it was the same as the powder she had put on his food. A strange spice that seemed to enhance the natural flavors of her womanhood a thousandfold. The realization that she had come fully intent on this happening dawned on him, and he smiled, happy to oblige.

He reached up to try hold her thighs, but she slapped his hands—hard. His cry was muffled by her weight pressing down.

"I did not give you permission to touch me," she scolded. She watched him lower his hands. "Good, now continue."

He stared up at her, unsure how he felt about her demeaning tone and actions. One on hand, he wasn't starved for affection; he didn't have to put up with this. On the other, it was excruciatingly hot. She had come here to be eaten out, prepared herself to make it enjoyable for him. Much like with tying up Ten, this was a game. He nodded and resumed his attention to her, using his tongue to part her lips and massage her inner sex.

She ground against him, her eyes half closing. Despite herself, she moaned, small sounds of pleasure escaping trembling lips as she reached down to pull his hair and yank his head up, forcing his face into her. He didn't mind, loved every second, sucking on her flesh. Her wetness dripped across his face as he worked his tongue in tight circles, flicking against her clit before sucking once again.

Her hips bucked hard, and for a moment, he was worried she would break his nose, or suffocate him, but what a way to go. Tentatively, he placed a hand on her right thigh and the other on her waist, her smooth, soft skin warm to touch. His cock ached, feeling like it would rip his pants right off of him any second. He ignored his ache as he saw to her pleasure. She continued to ride his face, her movements becoming less coordinated and more frantic with each passing second. He followed her direction, drawing arcane symbols of pleasure with the tip of his tongue and letting her moans guide him to her orgasm.

She let out a shuddering moan as she came, throwing her head back and arching her back. The sweet taste of her orgasm filling his mouth, he swallowed so he could breathe and dropped his hands, worried that as she came to her senses, she would punish him for touching her again. Slowly, she came to a stop. She wiped the sweat from her brow and pushed her hair out of her face, looking down at him between her legs as she fell back onto his chest.

"Good boy," she repeated.

Dhalius didn't respond—his jaw ached, and his face tingled—instead, he merely enjoyed the view of this ravishing Elven woman straddling his chest. Slowly, she untangled herself from him and rose, reaching for her pants. Dhalius slowly sat up himself, rubbing his jaw. He glanced up at her dressing and decided to press his luck.

"Thank you, Mistress," he said.

She shot him a look, and for the first time—including as she rode him—smiled. Though he wouldn't exactly call it a kind smile, he would take that as a victory.

"You are welcome, human." She pulled her pants on and, without another word, stalked out of his tent.

SHIELDS AND STAFFS

DHALIUS WAS WOKEN from his tent by the sound of a lone trumpet's cry. He rose quickly and dressed. The strange taste of whatever Palaas had used to enhance their nocturnal coupling lingered on his tongue—it wasn't unpleasant. Dhalius threw on his robes—the heavy fabric felt good to wear again after so many days out of it—and chained his book around his waist. Finally, he grabbed the staff and tucked it into his chain belt before heading out.

The camp was coming alive all around him. Women were shaking off sleep as they emerged from tents, already buckling armor and strapping weapons on. There was an excitement as well. They all knew what the sound of the horn meant; it meant action. Dhalius had to admit he shared that thrill. The knotted feeling in his chest, the nervous anticipation. It all meant the same thing. Soon, they would be throwing themselves at Goana's Rotting Eaves, and by all the gods of Magic and Life, the Defiant Host would *crush* them. He would prefer to spend more time training with the clerics, but he was excited nonetheless.

He followed the throng of warriors through the camp to the briefing area where Lakista stood. She looked haggard, as though she had not slept. Seeing the normally composed and stoic captain looking so disheveled was disconcerting, and he could hear whispers from other soldiers echoing his own sentiments.

"Hey, Dhali," Henri said, moving beside him. She wrapped one arm around his waist in a quick hug and then peered up at him. "Any idea what's happenin'?"

"Not yet," he said, frowning. "But from the looks of it, it's something serious. I've never seen the captain looking so . . . " He searched for a word that would encapsulate how she looked without sounding too harsh.

"Like shit?" Henri asked, pulling a laugh from the mage.

"Well, I wasn't going to say it like that, but yes." He glanced down at her, admiring the way the early morning sunrise played off her honey-colored braids. He needed to get back to Joachima and Bolokt after this briefing, to ensure the armory and the small cavalry were prepared for the coming battle. Then he should meet up with Ten to ensure they had everything they needed. Perhaps he should go to the Sanctum tent too. Tensions were high during training; perhaps a peace offering was in order.

Henri caught him staring at her, something he hadn't realized he was doing. "Can I help ye?" she asked with a grin.

"Just thinking how lovely your hair looks, and how lucky I am to have you watching my back in battle," he said, the feeling of easy affection and camaraderie warming his heart.

She blushed in response to his compliment and slapped his back, hiding her embarrassment with roughhousing.

"Ye charmer, ye!" she chided, then glanced past him and waved as Korska, Gisla, and Tawna as they approached.

Dhalius was about to greet them when the captain's voice rang out over the assembled masses of soldiers.

"ATTENTION!"

The entire Host, minus Dhalius, spoke in unison, crying out "Captain" and snapping their attention forward. Dhalius felt a little embarrassed to not know this particular call and response but ignored it, focusing his attention on the stage where the captain and her lieutenants stood.

"We received word last night that we are not facing the main force of the Rotting Eaves." She spoke quickly to cut off any murmurs of confusion. "The force we have been battling has been a splinter of their main cult-army. Currently, their main force is marching on Kandan." A massive cry went up at this. Kandan was the capital city of the Estherfel empire. Seat of the king, home of the Academy, base of the Mercenary Guild. There was likely not a single member of the Host who did not have friends or family in the city.

Lakista waited for the outcry to die down and raised a hand for silence. "I know. But do not lose heart. The Rotting Eaves faces the combined might of Estherfel's armies, several mercenary armies, and the people who taught our own battle mage."

Dhalius felt a blush creeping up his throat for being called out once again at a briefing, but instead of outrage and dirty looks, this time, it was met with a few cheers. Henri clapped him on the back, encouraging him.

"We have received no requests or orders from the Guild, which can only mean one thing," Lakista continued.

"That they want all the glory for themselves?" Korska shouted.

Lakista smiled, though her smile was a weary one. "I was thinking it meant they had things well in hand," she corrected. "But though ours is not the battle for Kandan, though we will not see the action that protects the throne, ours is still an important fight! What is a kingdom but its people? We fight for the people of Zachman's Crossing. We also know who leads this splinter. I won't say her name; you all know it."

She paused, letting the ripple of outrage and anger flow through the Host. She was a masterful orator, Dhalius realized; this was why she was the captain. She could stoke the fire in the hearts of her soldiers, leading them to hell and back on her words alone.

"So we fight for Zachman's Crossing. We fight for Estherfel. We fight for . . . *revenge!*" She cried the last word out, raising her sword in the air.

This time, Dhalius did not miss the cue. He, along with the rest of the Host, raised his weapon and cried out in a jubilant roar.

When the cry died down, Lakista cleared her throat. "I want all sergeants to the command tent. Once our plans are solidified, your sergeants will bring the battle plans to their squads. Eat and warm your sword arms, women. The Host marches for battle." She raised her sword again, eliciting another cry from the Host, before she walked off stage.

Korska grinned and looked between her squadmates. "I'll be back. I'll get us something good near the front."

"Try to make sure we're near the Elves and the clerics," Dhalius said. "We trained that hard, we should make use of it!"

Korska nodded and swatted his butt with a solid slap. "We'll see if Palaas and Estefani feel the same, but I'll do what I can. You lot get ready." She gave them all a lopsided grin before turning to trot off after the captain.

Tawna nodded her greeting, oddly quiet, but her being cold blooded, Dhalius assumed the early morning chill had her feeling sluggish. Gisla seemed to notice too. She wrapped an arm around Tawna's waist and nuzzled her, sharing her warmth with the Draconid. "Let's go. I'll heat you up," she said as she gently led the reptilian woman away. Dhalius watched them curiously, he had, of course, seen them coupling, had joined in on an occasion or two, but this had seemed more intimate. He wondered if their relationship went beyond sisters in battle and occasional lovers.

"Don't stare. It's rude!" Henri said, grabbing his arm and dragging him towards mess. Dhalius allowed himself to be dragged, though *allowed* was probably not the right word. Even Henri's light grip and tug was enough to overpower him, and he wasn't a weak or scrawny man.

Dhalius waited until they had grabbed what food was on offer, remnants of last night's stew thickened with oats and a piece of fruit, before asking, "Henri, can you tell me more about Goa—" He stopped when she shot him a warning look.

"Bad luck te say the name o' traitors," she said, her spoon slowly stirring the gruel to release steam and cool it off. "But I suppose it's best if ye know. What with ye bein' our secret weapon n'all." She took a bite of her pear and sighed. "She were the leader o' casters. Strong sorceress in her own, ye know? She claimed te be an entropy mage. S'pose that turned out te be another lie."

It made sense to Dhalius; it was the best lie that a necromancer could use to disguise the nature of their magic to other casters like the clerics. There was a fine line between the entropomancers and the necromancers. The only real difference was that the former liked things to stay dead and tended to form relationships with decomposers and carrion animals.

"Was she well liked?" he asked

"Eh." Henri shrugged. "S'hard te say. I think we mostly felt bad fer her, what with the disfigurement an all."

"Disfigurement?" he asked, confused. The woman who had visited him that night had shown no signs of disfigurement; she had been ravishingly beautiful. But given that she had been messing with his mind, he supposed she could have appeared however she liked.

"Oh aye!" Henri said. "The woman's papa locked her an' her family up and burned down their house te run away with his mistress, or so she says anyway. She grew old and frail, masterin' her magic while on the run from people who hated her fer her scars. That's the story she tol' us. No wonder that the old captain took her in—exactly the sort of sob story we go fer here in the Host." She sighed and pulled a flask from her hip, taking a swig and offering it to Dhalius. He took it and took a small sip so as to not insult her.

"That's horrible," he said, surprised to hear she was apparently much older than the vision he had seen.

"Aye, if any o' it is true." Henri shrugged and put her flask back, now diving into her stew. "Anyway, she traveled with us lots, a few years, made herself invaluable, was like a ma to many o' the girls. Hell, my own momma considered her a dear friend. But"—Henri's grip on her spoon tightened, and her knuckles turned white—"during the battle of Fralt, she turned on us. The dead rose at her whim and attacked us, dragging so many of the Host away to be sacrificed in some terrible ritual. We had to retreat, a complete disgrace. The captain and Ashakat did some diggin'. She had been plannin' it from the start. Poisonin' the old captain, manipulatin' others, creating the perfect conditions fer her li'l betrayal." Henri hung her head. "Fuckin' disgraceful." He could see her own bitter anger at having been fooled.

Dhalius leaned forward, placing his hand over hers. "This is not anyone's fault but hers, and we will make her answer for it."

"You will," Henri corrected, turning her hand to take his and squeeze it gently. "Yer twice the caster she could e'er hope te be. Ye'll drag 'er back te the Host in yer ink chains, bound and gagged. And Captain Lakista will mount 'er withered head on a pike as a warnin' to all who would try te betray us."

"*We* will, Henri. I can't do it without you," Dhalius said with what he hoped was a warm smile.

She returned the smile and pulled away from the table, grabbing her now empty bowl. He was always amazed how quickly she could put food away. "I'm glad ye joined us, Dhali, glad ye joined our squad. This next battle? We'll make that bitch sorry that ye did." She winked at him and left him to finish his own food.

No sooner had she gotten up than Palaas sat across from him once again. He stared at her for a moment, unsure how he was supposed to interact with her. She met his stare with her own, giving nothing away. She leaned forward and sprinkled some of that strange powder over his food. He glanced at it and then up at her.

"Thank you . . . Mis—"

She cut him off with a quick shake of her head, the ghost of a smirk playing across her lips. It was almost like a maiden offering a knight her shawl to remember her by as he rode off into war, but in this case, the maiden was riding alongside him and killing in cold fury. She rose without a word, no derogatory comments, no sneers. He watched her go and finally turned back to his own food.

"You got more!" Ten said as she jumped onto the bench next to him. He sighed, wondering if he would ever be allowed to eat, or if Ten had been watching and waiting for his food to get tastier.

"Would you like to share?" he asked halfheartedly.

"You are too kind, good sir," she said in a strange approximation of a noble human's halting speech patterns. She grabbed the spoon out of his hand and dug in.

He felt his irritation fade as he remembered how the clerics had looked down on her for what she was. But the Goblin's exuberant nature and the way she had no real concept of space, decorum, or property was frankly refreshing after the years of stuffy paranoia that ruled the Academy.

He grabbed the spoon back from her between bites. "I said share, not have, Ten," he chided with a grin before digging in to enjoy the fruits of last night's labors.

SHIELD AND STAFFS

KORSKA HAD GATHERED the squad, and they marched with the Host towards the oncoming armies of the Rotting Eaves in formation. True to Korska's promise, they were near the front lines. Unfortunately, that meant he was nowhere near the other casters. They were, as Korska put it, too squishy to be much good in a melee. And he couldn't disagree. They had fared well against the Elves in training, especially when Korska and Tawna were disrupting the Elves' efforts. But as soon as they had to content with both Dhalius and the warriors, there was little hope for them. Still, he was a bit disappointed—feeling the proximity of other mystics nearby, even if their magic was so different than his own, had been a strange comfort.

Thinking of them, Dhalius closed his eyes as he marched. Allowing his arcane senses to flow outward, he reached back, brushing against the presence of the clerics who marched near the captain. Now that he was opening himself up to it, he could feel not just them but the magical races of the Host as well. Gisla's warmth was most obvious, but he could also feel the Dryads and Elementals. He felt a small brush against his awareness, one of the clerics noticing him and acknowledging him.

"You okay, Dhali?" Henri asked, looking up at him.

"Yes, Henri, thank you." He realized he must have looked odd walking with his eyes closed. "I was using magic to check on our more magically inclined friends and allies. I can sense magical creatures and other magic-users."

"You can?" Gisla asked; she looked startled and discomfited.

"Yes, you can't sneak up on me." He smirked. "Only if I concentrate and I am looking, Gisla. If I was capable of sensing all magic at all times, it would be very overwhelming. It's also not entirely safe for me. If I can sense them, they can in turn sense me." He shrugged.

"So you couldn't use this ability to scout ahead and see what the other army has?" Korska asked.

"No, it wouldn't help. I would be overwhelmed by the undead, which each have some necromantic magic to their being. We already know they have necromancers. I may be able to figure out where on the battlefield Goana is, though. She used magic near me, on me. I know the taste of it."

Henri screwed up her face. "What does it taste like?"

"Not good. Like biting into an apple that looks good from one side and discovering it has rotted completely just behind the skin. Mealy and sour."

"How soon can you attempt to locate her?" Korska asked. "If we could send a ranger or scout ahead, we could cut off the head before the beast can even rise."

Dhalius shook his head. "No, as I said, I'll be closing off my senses as we get closer, not opening them further. I want as little contact with their magic as I can manage. It will already be pressing in all around us. Our best bet is to crush them."

The Defiant Host formed up, the formation flowing through highly regimented plans designed by company strategists to minimize weak points in the army and utilize its strengths. Dhalius didn't understand the ins and outs of it, but Korska seemed to. She stood proud, decked out in her platemail, her axe at her side. She looked majestic, and Dhalius was glad he was by her side rather than across the field from her. Henrietta stood on his other side, her scale mail shined to a polish, a warhammer taller than her in hand. She glanced at Dhalius and smiled grimly. Across the field, the moaning multitudes of the Rotting Eaves shambled forward, guided by their terrible masters.

Dhalius saw no war-beasts in their number, nor catapults or ballista—a small blessing, all things considered. But that did not mean this would be easy. Somewhere out there was a monstrously powerful wild-witch. A self-taught necromancer that had already dealt a deadly blow to the Host once before.

Captain Lakista's voice suddenly rang out over the sounds of the army's movements. "Who are we?"

"WE ARE DEFIANT!" came the roaring reply.

"When the odds are against us?" she called.

"WE ARE DEFIANT!" the army called back.

"When the world is at our throat?"

"WE ARE DEFIANT!" they shouted, joined now by Dhalius. Weapons slammed into shields; boots stomped.

From her war horse, Lakista pointed her sword towards the horde of the Rotting Eaves. "When the enemy demands our death?"

"WE. ARE. DEFIANT!"

The shockwave of three hundred women screaming their rage and bloodlust into the air as they began their charge shook the earth. Dhalius lifted his spell book, his inkbrush rising as he pulled the arcanely charged ink off the pages. Seconds later, they clashed into the decaying arms and rusted weapons of their foes.

No strategy can survive contact with a foe. Dhalius worked his way through the undead they faced. The implacable monsters fell under the razored whip of ink that flowed from the tip of the brush. The power flowed through his tattoos now, ebbing and flowing with his motions. Around him, Squad Korska was a battering ram through the moldering ranks of zombies, slowing only so they did not become separated from the rest of the army.

Above them, undead things flew through the air only to be lanced by the pinpoint accuracy of Elven arrows. On the ground, explosions threw up clouds of dirt and debris, the mad cackle of Ten-Tulips echoing faintly under each terrible boom. Tawna spun her twin maces around, calmly crushing bones and skulls as they came within her reach like a whirlwind of crushing steel.

"This feels like a feint," Korska shouted above the din.

Dhalius didn't answer, as he was focused on the middle distance, forcing a stream of ink down a necromancer's throat and then causing it to rapidly expand, ripping the disgusting man in half. He pulled the ink back and reached out to catch a leaping skeletal hound out of the air before it landed on Tawna, then flung it across the battlefield. She was right; the Host was ripping through the ranks of the undead with too little effort.

"Cover me!" he shouted and dropped to his knees. He brought the brush to his chest and arched his back as he allowed arcane energy to flow through him, the tattoos on his body crackling and illuminating with a blinding violet light. An inky miniature dragon formed above him, flapping its wings to soar above the battlefield, carrying Dhali's consciousness with it. He could see his body there, glowing with power, and how it acted as beacon for the undead. He could also feel them down there, the necromancers, and there was something wrong. Too few, too weak, and, most distressing of all . . .

Dhali snapped his eyes open as something pulled the brush out of his hands. "She's not here! Goana isn't on the battle—" He choked on his words as he saw that Henrietta was held with a blade to her throat by none other than Tzacha, the Dryad he had worked with to save the prisoners. In her other hand, she held the Staff of Viscu, still dripping with his ink. Around him, his squad was trying to fight to get to her, but the undead were threatening to overwhelm them.

"Tzacha . . . why?" he choked, reaching a hand toward Henri. "Don't . . . don't hurt her," he whispered.

"Why? Because death is a part of the cycle. Goana understands this. This world worships life and shuns death. She will bring about a glorious new world, one that is not choked by all the sentience that tries to bend the natural cycle to its whims."

"She's in your head, but you can fight it, Tzacha; let Henri go," he said, slowly rising from his knees, his hand outstretched. "Just let her go."

"She isn't controlling me, human. I have served her for decades, and I will continue to until we bring about the death of everything to finally make way for rebirth. You are pathetic, all of you. You will defy nature no longer. You will defy death no longer." And with those words, she dragged the blade across the Dwarf's throat, ripping it open. She stepped back smiling as the woman sank to her knees and toppled over.

"Henri!" he screamed, leaping to her.

He cradled her head in his lap, desperately trying to staunch the flow of blood. She reached up weakly, grabbing his hand. They both knew there was no saving her. The wound was too deep, too savage. Her time was measured not in minutes but seconds. He stroked her cheek, staring down at her, feeling the grief lodged in his chest choking his heart and lungs, making him feel as though he might lie down and die with her. He gently stroked a strand of honey hair out of her face and bent over to kiss her forehead. Even in that moment, she was brave, showing no fear of the death that approached, and then she was gone, her hand going lax in his.

"You should have followed the Mistress while you had a chance," Tzacha said, stepping back into the throng of the undead with a cruel smile on her face, assured in her victory and escape.

Dhalius's head snapped up, his eyes blazing with violet light. He lifted his hand, and a blade of ink snapped out and ripped the brush from the Dryad's hand. "And you should have killed me when *you* had the chance."

His mind was overwhelmed by the brush. It sang to him, promising him the world, promising him everything if he would just let it be unleashed. It was arguing with itself, begging for mercy and temperance, then begging for bloodshed. But a single word etched in his mind boomed across his psyche. *Vengeance.*

"Die," he growled.

Arcane ink and black energy shot from the brush, hitting the traitorous Dryad full force. She was lifted off her feet and flung through the air, but her body did not hit the ground. The power ripped at her, separating her limbs and head from her torso and then dissolving each part in the blast. And still it did not stop. Like a giant's scimitar crashing through the battlefield, it fell, tearing through flesh and earth alike. Spikes of red magic, red lightning that hurt the mind as much as the eyes to look at, cracked from the spreading inky blackness, lancing through the dead and their masters alike, turning them to charred ashen statues. Those that could scream in pain were left that way, silent screams on crumbling faces, until gravity caused them to fall apart. Dhalius's mind fell into the inky abyss he had summoned.

Dhalius was floating in nothingness, a white void empty of all sensation. And then, warmth.

"You can't give in to it," a voice said, surrounding him. "And I know it is so, so very easy to." A figure coalesced from the light. A younger man, but one who wore the worn smile lines of someone used to laughing, stepped towards him. He wore a shimmering robe of gold, white, and green, the symbols of Fele'na glowing faintly in the fabric.

"Viscu," Dhalius said. "Am I dead? Swallowed by your damned staff?"

"No. Not yet," the young priest said, stopping in front of him.

Dhalius found himself no longer in a void but in a grand temple. All around, plants grew. It wasn't so much that they appeared—one moment they weren't there, and the next, they always had been.

"But it is a danger. I can only protect you for so long, against so much."

"But why are you? Protecting me, I mean." Dhalius looked down at himself and was surprised to find he wore the same radiant Felenian robes as well.

"Because he must be stopped," he said gently. "The other one, the one whose touch is death and hate. Whose pain overshadows reason. She is already lost. With two pieces of my staff, he reaches into her mind constantly, pushing her to a path of ruin. Not just for her but for all the world. If you were to give in to him as well . . . all would be lost. And every sacrifice would be meaningless."

"But I am no saint. I am just a man, a lost man," Dhalius said, sinking to his knees.

"I wasn't a saint either. I was . . . not a fantastic priest," Viscu said, sitting next to him.

"You're known as a saint now. You alone held back Ektam; you alone defeated him and banished him. I'm not you," Dhalius said.

"No, not alone. I was with my lover, a soldier whom I traveled with . . . He and I, well, there is little in the world that love and lust cannot overcome. It was only with him by my side that I was able to banish Ektam. It saddens me that the world forgot my love. The church lies to lift themselves up, but in doing so do the greatest disservice, not only to my love but to the world. You are just a man, but you are not alone. Only through bonds of kinship and love, lust and compassion can you hope to overcome Ektam and his emissary."

The Felenian saint looked away, a wave of pain crossing his face. "We are speaking now because *he* is with her, speaking to and through her. His attention is elsewhere, and I am no longer capable of fighting his will in her heart. That battle is lost." Viscu looked saddened by the idea of Goana's damnation. "The war is just beginning, but it will be over before we have any chance if you give in."

Viscu took Dhalius's hand and brought it to his face, pressing his cheek against his palm. "I can feel your despair, the sense of loss. But I can also feel how strong your love is, how passionate you are. And I have felt them as well; they come to you because *they* can sense it. If you feel as though you cannot fight this battle for yourself, then do it for them."

Dhalius crumbled into himself. He was so tired. Every ounce of energy, of his very being, was drained. But he knew there was only one answer he could give. For everyone in the Host, for Henrietta, he nodded.

"He's alive!" someone shouted.

Dhalius opened his eyes. He was still there, kneeling on the battlefield, Henri's head resting almost peacefully in his lap. Smoke rose from his body, and his skin ached angrily around his tattoos. Around them, the undead were toppling over, their controlling warlocks dead or dying and the spells that animated them dissolved. Their living soldiers, cultists and brigands all, were scrambling to defend themselves against the fury of the unleashed Host. Gisla knelt beside him, staring at him in some mixture of awe and fear, while Korska towered above them, her axe swinging at any who dared get close enough.

The fighting continued, but it was merely cleaning up those faithless fools who had thrown in their lot with the Rotting Eaves. The battle was won, though Dhalius did not know if his heart could take the cost.

GRIEF AND KIN

T HE MARCH BACK to camp was somber. The captain had scoured the battlefield searching for Goana until Dhalius had pulled himself away from Henrietta's body long enough to break the news that the master necromancer had never been present at all. Bitter and angry, Lakista had ordered the enemies' bodies burned and the casualties of the Host readied for transport back.

Dhalius and Korska carried the stretcher with Henrietta on the march back. Gisla and Tawna were called to help with another of the fallen. They marched in silence, the pall of loss hanging heavy over their heads. Those squads that had lost no members, those of the Host who had lost no friends, they still felt beaten down by the fact that their target was nowhere to be found. The Defiant Host had needed to end Goana, to put her in the ground and pay her back for the stark betrayal they had faced at Fralt.

Instead, they marched back after a hollow victory, faced not with closure but with new treachery. Tensions were high as the women considered who else might serve Goana in secret, who else was merely biding their time. Dhalius did not consider these things as he walked the dusty road back to camp, his eyes dead ahead, the wooden handles of the stretcher biting into his hands. He had other questions. Why had Tzacha let him get the staff in the first place? Why the pageantry of being captured? She could have absconded with the staff and done away with both

Dhalius and several members of the Defiant Host's leadership back during their foray into the ruins.

There were only three options. The first was the simplest; Tzacha had been controlled by Goana. She had already proved she could tamper with someone's perception. But he dismissed that. He had searched for the sorceress, been looking specifically for her magic when Tzacha attacked. If the witch had taken control of Tzacha, he would have felt her.

Second, that was not Tzacha. There were various creatures and spells that could disguise a being. Could the creature that killed Henrietta be an impostor? Dhalius tried to remember how her aura had felt and what happened to her body as it was being torn apart by the out-of-control magic. But he had known only rage and grief in that moment, and the details escaped him. And *if* that were the case, what had become of the real Tzacha? It was both a comforting thought and a terrifying thought all at once. If the killer had not been Tzacha, it meant they were not betrayed. It also meant there could be other impostors. The difference between a traitor and the subterfuge of shape-shifters was nearly nil. The key difference was they would be able to root out those whose flesh was a lie much easier than those whose lies laid in their hearts.

Finally, there was something to be gained from Dhalius retaining the staff until now. Back during the rescue, he had wondered why Tzacha had not taken the shot. He had encouraged it; he had seen the cold calculations in her mind. Sacrificing him would mean she could go free. But was it all an act? And why had they kept the prisoners alive long enough to be rescued? The brute had made his lewd suggestions, but necromancers rarely had such lustful thoughts, their passion as dead as their nerve endings. Had the entire taking of prisoners and keeping them all been a ruse to move the pieces of the chess board into place?

His mind turned over the problem. Tzacha and Neela had been close as well. He remembered Neela's vulnerable night after he had returned with the women. Her gratitude had been real, making Tzacha's betrayal all the more brutal. What, then, had been the point of this? Had Goana needed Dhalius to wake the staff's power? Or maybe it was simpler than that. Maybe it was not Goana's play but the dark intelligence of Ektam. With Viscu's attention turned towards protecting Dhalius as he engaged with the relic, Ektam could cement his dominance over the necromancer, turning her from a power-hungry vassal into an empty vessel ready for his rebirth.

And now that Ektam controlled Goana, he needed the last piece of the staff to complete his resurrection and resume his subjugation of the kingdoms. It was a chilling thought. The full weight of a dead god's attention would be on him, and on the Host.

It was these thoughts that occupied Dhalius as they made their way back into camp.

Dhalius set down Henrietta as gently as he could, in line with all the other bodies of the lost. Among the bodies, he saw the body of one of the clerics, her features twisted into a mask of agony by whatever spell had felled her, and the broken form of an Elf ranger, her torso carved by three ragged claw marks. The wounded who could walk helped carry those who could not towards the med tent, and he started towards the forge.

"Dhalius," Korska called, taking two long strides to catch up and gently grabbing his shoulder. "Where are you going?"

"To Joachima, I have to—"

"No," she said firmly. "You don't. As sergeant of our squad, the responsibility is mine and mine alone." Her golden eyes were filled with kindness, but there was no compromise in her face. She would do this task, and she would do it on her own. "Go back to your tent, change, wash, be prepared to send Henri and the others off this evening. Those are your orders. That is . . . that is what you must do." She looked like she wanted to say something else but chose to remain silent as she passed him, making her way to tell a mother her child was gone.

Alone in his tent, Dhalius broke down. It was not just Henri's death that wore on him, though hearing Joachima's wail from across the camp tore his heart in half. It was the weight of it all. When he had finally felt accepted amongst the Defiant Host, he had felt such elation, such pride. But if he had never come, Henrietta might still be alive, and perhaps Viscu would have been able to break through to Goana. Beyond that, though, if he had not been assigned to this position, perhaps another, more capable mage would now be in his shoes, perhaps a mage who was up to the task of stopping Goana and Ektam. Instead it was him, and he was nothing but an adept of an obscure school of magic with little real-world experience.

He stayed in his tent, secluding himself, until Gisla showed up hours later. She pushed open the tent flap and looked at him, lying on his side on the cot, eyes red. "Come," she said. "We are going to give Henrietta the sendoff she deserves." And she left.

Dhalius rose. He didn't want to leave the tent; he didn't feel like he *should* attend. He did not feel as though he could face the captain, Joachima, or his squadmates. But it would be the height of cowardice to remain in his tent. It would dishonor Henrietta, and he would never do that.

He followed Gisla to the center of camp, where the bodies of the fallen were arranged in small pyres. The friends, lovers, and squadmates of the fallen were arrayed in a circle around each pyre. Dhalius moved to join Korska. He saw Joachima there as well but could not bear to meet her eyes. He knew he truly was a coward. Gisla stepped past them all to join Captain Lakista and Neela in the center of it all. Neela looked as cold and indifferent as ever, but there was an angry sadness emanating from her.

"We commend our fallen sisters to the great cycle. In

life, they were our comrades, our family, our loves, everything. We live because they protected us. We survive because they willed it. We honor their memory and sacrifice by being forever defiant of the evil that took them. We honor their lives by living ours to the fullest in their name." She paused and lowered her head. It was obvious she had given this speech many times, every time a member of her company was killed. Yes, despite knowing this speech by heart, it was not rote. Emotion filled every word of what she said. Dhalius realized that as furious and powerful as the captain was, she passionately cared about each of her soldiers. He realized he would go to hell to fight Ektam by her side, and he might just have to.

"Gisla," the captain said and clasped her hands behind her back.

Gisla nodded and stepped forward, dissipating into a living flame. Her body, a bronze shell, was left behind as her fiery essence spread to each pyre arrayed around them, lighting it and fueling the flames faster than any natural fire could ever hope to achieve. When each fire blazed, she coalesced back into her body and quickly joined Squad Korska beside Henri's body.

There, they stood as the fire burned, watching as it consumed their friend and comrade. He did not know how long he stood there, only looking away when he felt Joachima's hand on his arm. He turned and looked down, avoiding her gaze.

"Joachima . . . I cannot . . . I cannot begin to express." He choked.

"No, ye can't, not a soul could," she said and turned to face the pyre with him. "Ye know, we were talkin' about ye; I were teasin' her." She paused. "An she asked me, she asks, *'oi Momma, what would we do if I needed a dowry?'* Now, I know she were jokin'. But there is one." She paused, swallowing her sorrow as she tried to finish. "There is one that will never be used as such." She reached to her side and pulled a heavy-looking chain from her belt. It was beautifully shined, a strange metal that glinted. He had heard of Dwarven steel before, but it was a rare and expensive material, and it was rare to see it outside of the armory of high-ranking nobles or Dwarven lords. The chain loop was closed by a solid icon. It was shaped like an anvil that in turn was fashioned to look like a wolf's head. "That's the Vanberg crest there. My papa passed it to me, and I would be giving it to Henri when—Well it doesn't matter now." She held it up to Dhalius.

Dhali was struck by the enormity of the gesture, and it took everything in him not to choke on a sob. He shook his head. "Master Joachima, I . . . I can't. It's my fault Henri is gone. I can't take this."

"Don't ye ever say that again, boy," Joachima snapped. "She died a warrior protectin' what she believed in, protectin' those she cared for." She pushed the chain into Dhalius's chest, letting go as he reached up to hold it. "She would never blame ye, so donae ask me to either. Yer kin now. I christin' ye Dhalius Vanberg-LeReux. Do ye accept?" She spat it out, as though trying to race a typhoon of grief that was overtaking her.

He didn't understand Dwarven custom, but he knew in his heart this was how Joachima was honoring her daughter, this was how she was keeping her memory alive. She was in essence adopting Dhalius and commanding him to live and fight in Henri's honor and memory for the rest of his life.

"I do," he said softly. "With pride."

Joachima eyed him for a moment as if trying to ensure that he truly understood the enormity of what he was agreeing to, then nodded. She looked at the pyre again and then walked away into the night, hiding her proud tears from her comrades.

Dhalius considered following her, unsure if she should be alone at such a time. But he decided against it. He turned back to the pyre and nearly fell back. Palaas stood there in front of him. She glanced down at the chain in

Dhalius's hand and nodded thoughtfully before looking up into his face.

Her expressions were still alien to him, so difficult to read, but he thought she looked sad. She reached up wordlessly and gently grabbed the back of his head, guiding him down until their foreheads touched. Dhalius closed his eyes, accepting the gesture as one of sorrow and one of compassion. After a long minute, Palaas released him and walked away wordlessly.

Dhalius glanced back at the pyre. There was no sign of Henri's body any longer. He turned and began to move back towards his tent.

"Dhali," Korska called.

Dhalius turned to face her. She shook her head and took his hand. She stared into his eyes for several seconds before turning from the pyres and leading him away.

DEFIANT

KORSKA LED DHALIUS through the camp, and it wasn't until they stood amongst the tents that he realized she was leading him to the other squad members' lodgings. The largest was hers, made clear by an Orcish rune painted on the side. She pulled him inside the tent and finally stopped. The tent was larger than Dhalius's but sported less in the way of furnishing. A simple stand for her armor and weapons sat in one corner, and a footlocker for clothes sat next to piles of animal furs that covered the bare ground. She turned towards him and took the Vanberg chain from him, setting it down with loving respect on the footlocker before turning back to him and taking both of his hands in hers.

"Korska . . . " he started.

"Shut up," she said and pulled him into a tight hug.

He stood there for a moment and slowly returned the embrace, gently rubbing her back. Somewhere in his mind, he realized how difficult this was. The Host was filled with women who were damned and determined to never show weakness. And for Korska, an Orcish warrior, such feelings of vulnerability and weakness had to be an anathema. He slowly rocked with her as they held each other.

When she pulled back, he could see the tears in her eyes. For as much as he hurt, he could not imagine how much pain Korska was in. She had known Henri for years, had known her since the Dwarf was a child, had fought beside her in countless battles. He reached up and stroked

Korska's cheek, his thumb brushing a tear away. She watched him for a moment and then leaned down and pushed her lips against his.

It was not the passionate kiss of lovers who devoured each other hungrily in the throes of lust, but the hard and desperate kiss of a lost soul seeking comfort and connection. Dhalius returned the kiss, reaching up to cup her face and the back of her head as their kiss deepened. Slowly, they sank to the floor, unable, or unwilling, to break the kiss as they found themselves laying on the furs. Korska's left leg came up, wrapping around Dhalius's hip, pulling him tight against her, and his arms moved to her waist as he pushed her shirt up so his hands could gently stroke the skin of her waist and hips.

She broke the kiss, pulling back. Her eyes met his, filled with a terrible longing. She pulled at his shirt, biting her lower lip. He nodded and sat up so he could pull his shirt off. As it cleared his head, he saw she had already followed suit and had laid back to pull off her leather leggings as well. He watched her for a moment, taken by the sight her, before he pulled at his own trousers to get them off. Tossing them to the side of the room, he gently pushed her onto her back once her pants were off and resumed kissing, his teeth gently catching her lip and pulling.

He slid down her body, his face pressed against her chest, and he reached down between them to help guide himself between her legs. When he felt the press of her lips parting to accept him, he let go and placed his hands on either side of him, supporting himself as he used his knees to press into her. Korska gasped as he pushed into her, and then again as he slid in all the way. She brought her legs up, wrapping both around his hips, crossing her legs behind his back and using her legs to pull him in tight until they were flush.

He slowly moved against her. His mind was focused only on Korska, on being with her. He didn't consider pleasure, just the need to be connected, to be so close as to overlap. He brought one knee up to give himself more leverage and began a slow, rhythmic thrust, pushing himself up so he could look at her.

Korska reached over her head, her hands gripping the furs, a short gasp escaping her every time he ground against her. With one hand, Dhali reached down, grasping her left buttock and pulling it up off the floor, allowing him the perfect angle to meet her, sliding into her until their hips met. Sweat poured out of the two of them as they moved, each breathing hard, biting their tongues and lips to not spoil the moment with moans or words.

Dhali tightened his grip on Korska, a look of strained pleasure on his face as he tried to hold back. He didn't want this to end, he didn't want it to be over, but Korska's body would not stop moving, pulling him towards oblivion with her. Seeing his need, she brought her hands down to her sides and pushed herself up against him, meeting his lips in a deep kiss as they came together. Slowly, she sank back down onto the floor, and Dhali with her. He nestled his head against her chest, not pulling out or away. Every heartbeat pulsed an almost painful sensation through him as he twitched inside of her, and in turn, his spasms caused her to shudder with an intense pleasure.

Finally, he rolled off of her, nearly falling to the ground next to her. He faced her, staring at this beautiful woman who had shared this intense moment with him. She met his gaze and slowly moved down so she could pull him close into an embrace and kiss again. She threw a leg over his hips and nuzzled into his chest, only possible with them both lying down. Entwined as they were, they finally found sleep.

Over the next days, the Defiant Host packed up camp and began the long trek back to Estherfel. In theory, they had fulfilled their contract with Zachman's Crossing. The

Rotting Eaves force had been defeated, and the people of the city were safe. In practice, the company was eager to join the fight against the Rotting Eaves and their attack on Kandan. There was a general worry that should they arrive too late, they would miss the opportunity to kill Goana or someone else would claim her head. They traveled by day, and by night circled the wagons and set up just enough tents for basic necessities; the mess, the forge for any repairs needed, and, of course, the command tent. Before traveling for the day, Dhalius would assist Joachima with any repairs needed or Bolokt with re-shoeing the horses before they resumed their march. One day, he was called to the command tent.

He entered in his work clothes, though he now wore the chain of Vanberg around his waist, his spell book attached to it, the old chain lying at the bottom of his chest with his books. He stood with his arms clasped in front of him a couple of meters away from Lakista's desk, waiting for her to finish what she was working on and address him.

Lakista glanced up, taking in the man before her. What a far cry he was from the green youth who had first been foisted upon her. He had tanned from his work in the forge and stables, his hair lightened by the sun. He was also more sure of himself. He looked less like a confused Academy graduate and more like an officer of war. The Crest of the Defiant Host was just visible under his collar, and the spidery arcane tattoos that went from his temple to his right knuckles were now all healed. But she saw he now sported fresh tattoos on the left arm as well. Dwarven sigils and runes had been drawn though his flesh by the spinner from elbow to knuckle. She recognized them as the clan markings of Vanberg.

Finally, she sat back and looked at him over steepled fingers. "Dhalius Vanberg-LeReux."

"Captain," he acknowledged, though he was fairly certain this was the first time she had called him anything other than *mage*.

"That last battle. You lost control again." It wasn't an accusation; it was just a statement.

"No, Captain, in the last battle, I surrendered control."

"To get the staff back from Tzacha," Lakista said, nodding in understanding.

He wished he could let it lie. "No, I had the staff back in my hand. I surrendered control because I wanted to kill Tzacha for killing Henri. It was a choice, and one I will not make again." He swallowed. "It was the first time I've ever lost a companion in battle, the first time I ever saw a friend die, let alone in my arms. I was not ready for how much it hurt."

Lakista sighed and nodded. "Ah, that I can understand, but you feel confident you won't lose control again?"

Dhali thought of the vision of Viscu, the young man whose essence was trapped in the staff, forever waging war against a mad god, and about the priest's plea. "Yes, Captain. I am."

"Very well. I called you here this morning because you are causing me a dilemma," she said, gesturing to the paperwork in front of her. "Any other soldier in this outfit who single-handedly saw us to victory in two major actions would be promoted. Not just promoted but celebrated. They would be lifted up for rescuing hostages, for winning battles, for killing that fucking traitor. But . . . " She trailed off.

"But I'm a man."

"Precisely. And you've only been with us for a short while. Promoting you would be a slap in the face of every woman who has sacrificed just as much as you have to be where they are. On top of that, it would send a signal to the world. It wouldn't matter that you earned the accolades; all they would see is that a man joined the Host and then shot up the ranks immediately. While I am not one to give a fuck about what others think, it would be damning to our reputation, to everything we have fought to achieve as free women."

Dhalius nodded.

"You see my dilemma," she said.

"If I may, Captain?" he asked. She gestured for him to continue. "You say I single-handedly won battles, and that just isn't the case. Against the beast, I could never have gotten close enough if not for Palaas and her squad. Sure, I felled a monster, but for every one monster I killed, every other member of the company killed a score of enemies. My kill was flashier, more theatric, but again, even that, I could not have done alone. And in our last battle, and with killing Tzacha. Ten's bombs did just as much damage as I did. The rangers kept the flying monstrosities raining down around us harmless, and without Korska and her squad in all three of the battles I have fought in, I would be dead a hundred times over. I did nothing single-handedly. I may have been the blade that struck the decisive blow, but Korska, Palaas, and their squads are then the hilt, and you are the hand that pointed that blade. I need no accolades. I have no interest in a promotion, now or ever. I am content being a battle mage of the Defiant Host."

"You are sure?" she asked, tapping the sheet of paper in front of her—he could see now that it was a log book for the coffers showing how much each mercenary was to be paid.

"I am positive, Captain."

"If you have any wishes, Dhalius, now is the time to ask while I am feeling generous," she said with a tight-lipped smile.

"Well, I would ask that you allow me to help train the Host in better dealing with magic-users, especially the clerics. Goana sabotaged you so that you would be easier to pick off. I would like to correct that."

Lakista was about to answer when a loud commotion sounded from outside the tent. A moment later, Geoffrey Dennen pushed his way into the tent. He was scowling, but as soon as he saw Lakista, the scowl turned into a smug sneer. "Captain Lakista!" he said jovially.

"What are you doing here, Dennen? I didn't think to see you so soon after . . . last we spoke." She spoke carefully, avoiding antagonizing the man who might see them deployed far from the real fight. Turned out she needn't have bothered.

"I came to personally deliver a message to you from the throne of Kandan," he said with a small flourish.

Dhalius's heart ran cold. The man was too gleeful for it to mean anything good.

"What does good King Aste need with the Defiant Host?" she asked, crossing her arms over her chest.

"Good King Aste," Dennen said, his smile growing somewhat manic, "is dead. Kandan has fallen, surrendered to the invading army, and Empress Goana has ascended to the throne of Estherfel."

Both Lakista and Dhalius stood frozen, unsure how to process this terrifying news. While they had been out fighting for their lives and the lives of the innocent, the war had been lost?

"Hold on," Lakista said, holding up a hand. "How did Goana defeat both the armies of Kandan *and* the combined might of the Mercenary Guild and the Academy?"

"She didn't need to defeat the Mercenary Guild," he laughed. "She hired us. As for the Academy, it's amazing how few mages know how to dispel a dagger to the gut while they sleep. You may want to practice that one, *Master* Dhalius," he said with a conspiratorial wink.

"You traitorous dog!" Lakista said, rising from her chair.

"Traitor?" Dennen chuckled. "Please, we're mercenaries. We have always fought for coin, nothing else. Now, for the message. Deliver the fragment of the Staff of Viscu to her holy majesty and bend the knee, swear fealty and the fealty of your company to the crown of Kandan, and you will be allowed to live. Hell, you'll be allowed to thrive. Reject this offer and you'll be hunted by every resource at her disposal. And, Captain, her resources are *vast*."

Lakista looked down. He *was* technically correct. They were mercenaries; they fought for coin, not loyalty. She could guarantee the survival of the Defiant Host. She slowly removed her sword from the scabbard. She lay the blade and hilt flat across her palms and walked forward, offering the sword to Dennen. All she had to do was forgive a woman's sins and swallow her pride. She stepped up to the Guild official who had betrayed his kingdom for coin and dropped her hand suddenly, taking a grip of the hilt, and rammed the blade up and through Dennen's fat gut and up into his lungs.

She stared into his eyes, not blinking even as he coughed blood into her face. "Don't worry, I'll have your head delivered to Goana so she can resurrect you and receive our message from your fat slug lips," she hissed and pushed him off her blade and out of the tent, following after him as he stumbled and fell into the dirt.

A circle of women surrounded them, shocked at what they saw. Dhalius followed after.

Lakista stood over Dennen as he squirmed, dying in the dirt in the very center of camp. "Goana has taken the throne? She is arraying vast forces against us? Fine! Let any woman who fights solely for coin without conviction in her heart leave the company now!" Lakista called, her voice ringing out as clear and strong as the day she had led them into battle. "From this moment on, we are not a mercenary company in thrall to greed and petty squabbles. We are now the rebel army of Estherfel, and ever we remain defiant." Her blade fell, cleaving the head of Geoffrey Dennen from the body.

A roar filled the air as the Defiant Host affirmed their new calling. Underneath the roar, Lakista looked at Dhalius, grim determination etched across her features. "Your request is granted, Dhalius. Prepare us for what is coming."

Dhalius watched her march back into the tent and then looked at the body of the man who, just a few short months ago, had delivered him to *this* very tent. He felt no sorrow at the man's passing; he had chosen his path and his fate. And Dhalius had chosen his. He reached down and touched the Staff of Viscu, saying a silent prayer to the saint and to Fele'na. He spared one last look at the company banner that hung above the captain's tent, then turned to find Korska. There was no time to lose. The Defiant Host marched to war.

About the Author

Dez Zuri is an author of erotic fiction, romantasy, dark romance, and more. They live and write in Texas, striking out against the establish purity culture with steamy abandon.

www.ingramcontent.com/pod-product-compliance
Lightning Source LLC
Chambersburg PA
CBHW020040310726
48970CB00007B/2339